THE NEW KID'S REVELATION

A Domestic Fable

Marck Thomas Wilder

MOT JUSTE PUBLISHING

Paperback ISBN 979-8-9917284-1-6

Hardcover ISBN 979-8-9917284-2-3

Originally published in The United States of America by Mot Juste Publishing, 2024

THE NEW KID'S REVELATION

A Domestic Fable

Marck Thomas Wilder

Author Introduction

Let's talk real quick about stories.

They can be our greatest teachers, our harshest critics, our most trusted companions. And I'm not just talking about the silly nonsense tales you read your kids to help them pass out at bedtime, or the multiplex blockbuster revenge epic you catch on a Friday night, or the serialized dramas that keep you glued to your screen, hour after hour, gawking like witnesses at a ten-car pile up. While many good stories *can* serve as nothing more than an amusing escape into fantasy, I am not talking about those kinds of stories. I'm talking about the stories that burrow their ways deep down into us, shaping us and our worlds from the inside out, in ways that nothing else quite can. They are often our first teachers, teaching us, by example, how to be brave or clever, cautious or kind—as well as showing us the consequences of what happens when we are not. They can even serve as magic mirrors, in a way; granting us visions of who we are, who we want to be, and what we're afraid of becoming. In short, I believe that stories carry the divine, transcendent, and healing powers to show us what it means to be truly, deeply *human*.

I have always held a kind of sacred reverence for these kinds of stories, seeing them as a kind of secular scripture—the ways they slip into our hearts and minds, imparting wisdom about how to live in the world around us, and—perhaps more importantly— the worlds within us, connecting us with the deepest parts of ourselves and each other.

Consider the power of a simple fable—those timeless, bite-sized moral nuggets floating in the ether of our collective consciousness. These are some of the earliest meaningful stories we ever hear—whether Aesop, Jean de La Fontaine, or Dr. Seuss—acting like guiding signposts, each one pointing us in the direction of a particular truth or virtue or lesson, teaching us the differences between right and wrong in simple, easy-to-digest terms: *Don't lie. Don't be selfish. Don't be greedy.* But they're also quite *safe*, aren't they? *Tame.* They reassure us that, as long as we're good and doing what we're supposed to, then we can avoid folly and misfortune, and all will be well. But not all stories are quite so comforting.

Some stories show characters on an 'upward' journey—these are what we call "comedies" (and no, I don't mean comedy in the jokey, slapstick, laugh-out-loud sense of the word). We can think of a comedy as any story where the main character—after persistently facing down a series of obstacles and adversities—ends up in a better place than where they started. The hero slays the dragon, saves the kingdom, and lives happily ever after. Cinderella ditches her toxic family for a life of love and luxury. The lonely, downtrodden, and self-doubting character gets dragged into some strange world of adventure, and in doing so, they forge new, unbreakable friendships and learn just how much goodness they are truly capable of.

Comedies are the most common and popular stories we see and hear because these are the stories that get to have happy endings. These stories give us hope by showing us that, no matter how bad things get, there's always a light at the end of the tunnel; if these characters can meet their challenges head-on and come out better and stronger on the other side, then maybe—just maybe—I can keep going and, eventually, everything will turn out okay for me, as well. These stories are essential for reminding us that life—for all its hardship, loss, and suffering—is still, ultimately, *good.*

Unfortunately, life doesn't always take us on that 'upward journey' and not every story has a 'happy ending'. Sometimes, our beliefs, our choices, or our life circumstances can take us down a darker path, and these 'downward' story paths are known as "tragedies". These stories don't let us off the hook so easily, holding up a dark mirror to our own lives, reflecting back the parts of ourselves we'd rather not see, warning us about the nature of our own flaws and weaknesses. Here, the main character might start off with high hopes and dreams, but as the pages turn, so do their fortunes, and no matter how hard they try, things just seem to keep getting worse, with every new choice leading to more loss, more suffering, and more despair. In these stories, the main character rarely succeeds, the villains are seldom vanquished, and the lines between right and wrong become hopelessly blurred. Like fables and comedies, tragedies pack a powerful ability to teach us profound lessons about our own lives—the only difference being that tragedies teach by using a negative example, essentially saying: "Don't do what *they* did." While they are rarely ever as much fun as comedies, these stories are no less important, holding up a dark mirror to our own lives, reflecting the parts of ourselves we'd rather not see back at us, warning us about the nature of our own flaws and weaknesses, as well as the dangers lurking in the shadowy depths of our own hearts. Tragedies serve as a potent reminder that life is not always fair, that our thoughts and choices have consequences, and that sometimes—no matter how hard we try—things still fall apart.

It seems only fair to warn you before we proceed that, this story you're about to read, it leans more toward the *tragic* side. It's the story of a boy named Brennan, whose early path in life—like so many others'—is shaped by forces beyond his control or understanding, pulling him deeper into a world of suffering and confusion. It's a story of what happens when the people who are supposed to guide and protect us fail us instead. It's a story about finding one's way in a world that seems determined to drag us down, marked by internal struggles that many of us might recognize: the search for identity, the need for acceptance, the pain of discipline, and the sting of manipulation. It's a sad tale, to be sure, and as such, it is not the *easiest* read. While I have called this story a "*Domestic Fable*", please make no mistake: this is not some simple fantasy yarn with a tidy little moral at the end, nor does it follow the upward path of the comedy, with some guaranteed happy ending to comfort us at the end—but it's a potent story, and one worth telling, nonetheless.

Now, if you're ready, gentle reader, I invite you to turn the page, joining me and Brennan on this early stretch of his long life's journey. Just remember: Brennan's story isn't here to cheer you up or help you feel better about your own life—in fact, parts of the story might even make you feel quite uncomfortable—but I believe that the same stories that hit close-to-home and make us uncomfortable are oftentimes the ones we need to hear the most. And never forget that, as much as stories can wield the power to break our hearts, they have an even greater capacity to teach us, heal us, and—if read with the right kind of eyes—the right stories can even help teach us how we might heal others.

So, if you're looking for a story that will make you feel good, this might not be the one for you. But if you're looking for one that will make you think, make you feel, and maybe even see your own story a little differently by the time you reach the end— well, then maybe, my courageous friend, you are right where you need to be.

Thank you so much for reading,

- Mr. Marck

Table of Contents

One.

There was once a good little boy named Brennan, who spent much of his time alone, waiting for his parents to return home. They shared a modest home in one of the poorer corners of their big city—though the three of them were rarely ever all home and awake at the same time. Both of his parents had to work long hours, every day of the week—and often even on weekends—just to cover their basic household expenses, returning well after the sidewalk lamps dotted their dark street in patches of flickering orange. Yet, despite the long days apart, their return was always the highlight of Brennan's day; that rush of giddy energy during the final hours leading up to his bedtime when the entire house felt whole again.

Every morning, from the time the boy was old enough to walk into a classroom, he would wake himself up, get himself dressed, brush his teeth, and microwave a styrofoam cup of noodles for his breakfast—all while his parents were still sound asleep—then he would set out on the long walk to school, where he would always give the day's work his best effort.

Brennan loved all of his teachers, and they all loved him. They never told him outright that he was one of their favorite students, but he had a good sense of their affections based on their consistently kind and gentle treatment. They knew that he was a good boy and that he always made his best effort to sit still and listen quietly and attentively to their lessons—at least until he knew the answer to one of their questions (as he often did), then he would shoot his hand up into the air and wait patiently to be called on before announcing his best answer to the class. He was always polite and arrived on time, and even when he got answers wrong (which *did* happen from time to time), he wouldn't get upset with himself. Rather, he would simply wait until after class and politely ask his teacher to explain the *correct* answer, doing his best to learn and remember what she had told him, trying to figure out how he had made the mistake, as well as how he could avoid making that same mistake in the future.

Brennan's parents would both be at work by the time he returned home in the evening, but they had given him a copy of the house key to let himself in. Once inside the darkened house, he would turn the lights on and get himself a snack—usually a cup of milk and either a bag of chips or another cup of microwave noodles—then, after completing his homework and chores for the day, he would zone out in front of the TV for a couple of hours until one of his parents came home carrying either a big cardboard pizza-box or logo-emblazoned paper bags full of their evening's fast-food dinner.

As the parent—whichever one of them happened to return home first—entered the house and hung up their clothes, poured themself a drink, and set about plating their evening's dinner, they would often unwind by sharing their workday complaints and annoyances with their young son; all the little irritating or unfair habits of their bosses and coworkers, and all of the snappy insults or comebacks they *wished* they could have said to them. As far as the parents were concerned, they could have just as easily been sharing their feelings with a cat or a dog or a houseplant, as neither of them truly expected their son to provide any *real* solutions to the countless daily miseries they carried with them. But the boy had grown used to this little *after-work ritual* of theirs, and even though he never knew who any of these bosses or coworkers of theirs were, and could rarely ever follow along with the disjointed and emotionally charged sequences of events as they described them, he knew that they were letting out their feelings (or "*venting*," as his mother called it), and he wanted to do everything he could to be there for them and to help them feel better.

So every evening, Brennan would do his best to sit patiently and give his parents his full, undistracted attention—just like he did for his teachers—taking in every little gripe they had to say, and when they would occasionally pause after saying something like, "Can you *believe* that guy?!" or "You know what I mean?" the boy would respond with his best guess of what they wanted to hear, like, "Well, that's not fair at all!" or "You're absolutely right, mommy!" or, "That must'a made you so mad, daddy!"

But over time, the stresses and anxieties weighing heaviest on the parents' minds and hearts only grew heavier and more pressing. Every month, it seemed, their household bills and expenses kept increasing at higher and higher rates, but the money they earned from their jobs wasn't going up at all. They were already working hard and as often as they could. They never turned down an opportunity to pick up extra shifts on weekends, and tried to work every weekend they could—even pretending that they weren't feverishly sick when they actually were, just so they could keep on working as usual—but as hard as they tried, they simply couldn't find any other ways to make more money.

As the years passed and their stresses mounted, Brennan observed that his parents started turning their after-work frustrations against each other—rather than the people at work—and ranting about new grievances, like, "As hard as *I* work, you'd think the *least* your father could do is get the ladder out and clear out our gutters every once in a while—but no-o-o!" or "As hard as *I* work, you'd think the *least* your mother could do is make us a real home-cooked meal every once in a while—but no-o-o!" And on and on it went, day after day, with the parents sharing their innermost marital wishes and woes more comfortably with their son than they ever would with each other. Each time he heard them talk about each other that way, his heart sank deeper and heavier, yet he still did his best to nod along and agree with everything they had to say, uttering only small, vaguely agreeable grumbles in response, like, "*Mm...*" and "Uh huh..." and "Yeah... I guess..."

Without ever intending to, or even realizing it was happening, the two parents had grown into a pair of bitter and cynical people, and the more stress or pressure they were under at any given moment, the more the irritable, impatient, and annoyed they became—first with their jobs, then with each other, and eventually... With their son.

Two.

Before the third grade, Brennan's parents had only ever spanked their son on two separate occasions, several years before.

The first time was during one of the boy's earliest trips to a restaurant, when he was little more than a baby, barely starting to join words together into simple sentences. He had, up until that point, always been a well-behaved child when it came to his meal-times, and during the few restaurant outings they had taken him on before, he sat quietly and ate his food, taking in the scenery around him—but on this *one* occasion, a little tomato soup dribbled down the mother's chin and the boy burst into gleeful, shrieking laughter at the sight, clapping his hands with wide-spread fingers. He then shoveled a heaping spoonful of his own soup into his mouth and blew it sputtering all across the tablecloth between them, squealing the whole time. While the parents both shot up from their seats—their faces reddened by anger, embarrassment, and flecks of soup—their baby boy found the whole spectacle uproariously thrilling. He raised his pudgy little hands, squealing in celebration, and brought them both splashing down onto the outer lip of his bowl, catapulting its thick red contents up into the air where it drizzled back down, spattering the tablecloth and their clothes in his dinner.

"Right," the father said, and swooped in, hoisting the giddy boy up out of his highchair. He dragged Brennan across the lobby by his wrist at such a furious pace that the boy's wobbly legs—only newly accustomed to walking—could hardly keep up, tripping and stumbling in his father's wake the whole long walk to the restroom.

The father guided Brennan into a stall with him and took a seat on the toilet. He scowled fire down into the boy's strained and quivering face, shooting hot jets of air out his nostrils with each breath. The boy was already terrified by that point, confused as to how his *funny dada* could have so quickly transformed into such an ominous figure—so much scarier than any nightmare he'd ever had—and hoping, more than anything, that the man's face would return to normal soon. The sight of his father's anger-warped face would stay with him, reappearing to torment him in dreams and dark rooms for years, filling his guts with a heavy, jagged feeling that he would be unable to recognize or describe for most of his life—despite its constant presence throughout.

Then, without a sound uttered between them, the father picked the boy up, flopped him over his knees, and gave Brennan three firm swats on his diapered bottom ("*Rela-a-ax...*" he would later tell the mother, upon returning to their table, "*It was no harder than I'd slap my own knee at a good joke.*"). Despite the cushioning of his diaper, each swift *whap* from the man's flattened hand shot a small, seismic jolt up the boy's nervous system, from his tailbone to the base of his skull, engulfing the boy's entire being in pain and frantic confusion.

The man propped Brennan back up to face him, digging his fingers into the boy's shoulders to hold him upright, as he was still woozy and weak-limbed from his ordeal—far too noodly to stand on his own and moaning a shrill whine with every spasming breath—and he said, "Hey... *Hey...* C'mon, *up here*— look at me," then he gave Brennan a shake that whipped his head from back-to-front and repeated his command, "Boy, you will *look* at me when I'm talking to you."

When Brennan could finally lift his shining wet face up to meet his father's loveless scowl, the man continued, "Now, what you just did in there was *un-acceptable*. It was *bad*—do you hear me? You were a very *bad boy* in there, and I *refuse* to have such a bad boy for my son. So I am going to leave you in here for as long as it takes until you can promise me that you will only ever be a good boy from now on. And when you think you're ready to make me that promise, then you can come out of here."

The father waited, leaning against the wall just outside of the men's room door, and a couple minutes later, the door cracked slowly open, just enough for Brennan to slide and waddle his way through. The boy sniffed back hard with each breath, choking and coughing up the fluids collecting in the back of his throat. Then, still pawing at his eyes with his soft knuckles, he looked up at the man and said, "I'll be a good boy now... I *pro-o-omise...!*"

—　　　—　　　—　　　—　　　—

The second time Brennan got spanked, he was out with his mother on a shopping trip. She had parked her cartful of goods next to her SUV and was fishing her keys out of her purse, when a lost and somewhat deflated balloon, hovering just above Brennan's eye-level, drifted past him and across the parking lot toward the road. Without thinking, the boy bolted after it, following the balloon out into the street. He was just reaching out with both arms to grasp it like a hug, when he was yanked back by the collar of his jacket, just in time to save him from the path of a speeding car.

The sudden reality of what had nearly happened struck him nearly as hard as that car would have, sending him into an instant fit of panicked wailing.

His mother spun him around to face her and shook his shoulders, flailing his head with each shake. "What is the *matter* with you? What're you, *stupid?* Are you *trying* to give your poor mother a heart attack? Did you really think a *balloon* was worth letting a car run you over? *Huh?* Is *that* what you thought? God, the *last* thing I'd need right now is for your father to find out that you almost got yourself killed while *I* was watching you—I would *never* hear the end of it! I mean, just *what* were you *thinking?!* You know, sometimes, kiddo, I just don't know what goes through that little pea-brain head of yours..." And on and on it went for the entire car ride home, as the boy sat in shameful, weeping silence.

Once inside the house, she told him, "I'm going to have to spank you now so that you'll remember never to run into the street without looking again."

"But I *will* remember, mommy—I *will!*" Brennan said. "I know that it was bad and stupid of me, and I feel so bad and stupid already, and I never want to feel like this again, or make you scared like this, ever, ever again—I *swear!*"

The mother sighed and shook her head. "No, *nuh-uh.* See, 'cause I'm worried that you really won't learn your *lesson* here unless you get punished. You do the crime, you gotta do the time... And besides, I'm *still* all shook-up and mad at you for what you did—I mean, just look at my hands!" She held her hands out between them, long enough for Brennan to see that they were, indeed, shaking. "So, *yeah...* Come on—you get over here, now... Let's just get this done and over with."

Unlike Brennan's father, who found it sufficient to give him three firm *whaps* over his diaper that previous time in that restroom stall, his mother, instead, swung him over her lap so that his feet dangled limp the floor and tugged his waistline all the way back down around his upper-thighs. Then she raised her arm out to her side and held it suspended there for a moment, and just as Brennan was beginning to wonder when the impact would come, or how much it might hurt, she drove her tensed palm down onto his bare bottom, fast as a karate chop, with all of her might.

On impact, Brennan's facial features all warped into a wet and throbbing mask of panic and pain, his face as glossy as a porcelain doll's, gasping and choking with each forced inhale, and then wailing with every exhale until his cries were replaced by raspy wheezing. Before he could recover from his mother's first whip-fast swat, she sucked in a deep breath and brought her rigid palm cracking down on him once more—then again, and again—repeating the process nearly a dozen more times before finally letting up, sweaty and out of breath. Her hand glowed the same deep shade of cherry blossom pink as Brennan's backside and tearslicked face, and it shot hot waves of pulsating pain out to her fingertips, as though a bee stung her palm.

"There," his mother said between panting breaths, wiping the sweat off her lip with her sleeve, "*Now,* I think you learned your lesson."

And for several years, those were the only two times his parents ever laid a hand on him.

Three.

One autumn evening, shortly after Brennan entered the third grade, his mother returned home after a *particularly* upsetting end to her workday—thanks to a *particularly* disgusting remark she received from one of her least-favorite male coworkers. She schlepped her way up the paved path that parted their lawn, rushing with the twitchy energy of someone racing to find a toilet, frazzled and fussing with the burdens she carried. She held her coat and scarf folded over one arm, clutching her keys and handbag in that hand, while balancing a large pizza box atop the other. She had only made it a few steps inside when, distracted by her own aggravated thoughts and not watching her step, she tripped over the school bag that Brennan absently dropped and left by the entrance when he first arrived home.

She instantly dropped the bundled load as that hand shot out to brace her tumble to the floor, but the hand carrying their dinner instinctively swung forward to join the other, launching the pizza box through the air, where Brennan watched helplessly—as though it was some TV scene playing out in slow-motion—as its lid popped open, releasing the sizzling pizza into a high arc, flipping end over end like a flapjack until it finally landed with a wet *slap*, crust-side-up on the tiled floor.

The next thing the boy saw was his mother's eyes flicking up to meet his own from under a hard-edged brow, her face tinted the color of her wrath, as she parted her lips, peeling them back over her clenched teeth into a vicious, grinding snarl.

"Oh, *mommy!* Oh, I'm so, *so* sorry, mommy! Are you okay? Are you hurt? *Ugh*, I'm *so stupid-stupid-stupid!* I should'a never left my backpack there! I'll never do it again, mommy; I *promise!* I'll be *good*, I'll... I'll hang it up every day—in my *room,* even! I *swear!*" Then, when she didn't reply, and just picked herself up while still staring angry holes into him, he added, "...And, maybe we can even, um... I mean... Do you think we can still *eat* it?"

Without another word between them, she stormed over, grabbing him up off the couch by his armpits and sitting herself down in his place, then slinging him over her lap and grabbing a fistful of his waistband, wrenching his pants down around his thighs while he squirmed and squealed, before—*WHAP, WHAP...* And that was all the spanking her throbbing hand could dole out before the hot, tingly pain from her awkward landing forced her to stop. She huffed and stretched out her fingers, shaking her wrist out a few times, then she shoved the boy back up onto his feet, making a disgusted face at him and snapping, "Pull your pants up—right now, come on, *come on!*" And the boy did as he was told. "Now," she said, "hold out your arm."

He hesitated, parting his lips to say something, but before he could utter a sound, his mother just held up her finger and shook her head. "No, no. Come on now. Your *arm. Now.* You were a *bad boy,* and you still need to be punished more. For all you know, I could have broken my neck just now! Is *that* what you want? *Huh?* Is that what you were *trying* to do—*break your mother's neck?!* Your actions have consequences, young man. And that's what you're going to learn today. *Now...* For the *last* time: your *arm.*" His whole body jolted when she growled the word, "arm," and his hand immediately shot out in front of him.

The boy stared down the length of his arm, whimpering and gulping, unsure of just what hopeless and painful fate she had in store for it.

"When *I* was a little girl, the nuns who taught at the school I went to, they had this big, scary paddle that they kept over the door for just this kinda thing—a splintery old wooden paddle as long as my arm, hung up there for everyone to see, with holes drilled into it like swiss cheese so that it could hit us even faster and harder than a regular paddle. Other times, other teachers, they might've had us kneel on some loose popcorn kernels while saying our prayers—sometimes for hours at a time... There was no end to the different ways they came up with to teach us the hard lessons that only ever come through strict, unflinching punishment... But not *you.* No, you're getting off *easy* tonight, kiddo. I'm just gonna give you a few little pinches here on your arm, and that should be that." She frowned and looked away for a moment, snorted, then resumed her business, adding, "Just like my mother used to give me, God rest her soul… Alright, now…"

She reached out and gripped a random lump of the boy's arm flesh between her thumb-tip and first knuckle, and proceeded to tighten that grip like a vice, twisting as hard as she could to maximize the pain.

"Ow, mommy—oh, *ow! Ow-ow-ow-ow-ow! Mommy! Okay, okay*—I think it hurts *too* much, mommy—it's too much, it's too *much!*"

"*Quit… Wriggling… Around…*" She lost her grip on his pinched skin and it snapped back flush with the rest of his arm, leaving a dark little blotch the color of unripened blueberries separated by a white crease along the spot where she pinched. The boy tried to hold a straight face for her, but tears were already streaking slick paths down his cheeks. "It'll only hurt more if you keep moving, wiggle-worm. Just stay there and take your medicine like a man—and don't you start crying just because of a few little pinches, or I'll *give* you something to cry about! Now come on, arm out. We're not done here yet."

The mother gave the boy another half-dozen pinches up and down his arm, from wrist to elbow, while the boy did his best to keep his eyes squeezed shut and stay perfectly motionless—save for the pained twisting and scrunching of his face, and an occasional sniff to hold his tears back.

"There… I think you've probably learned your lesson by now, don't you think?" the mother said, deciding the boy had finally had enough, "Now, go and clean up your mess on the floor there—and clean it quickly so we can run back out and pick up some dinner before your father gets home."

—   —   —   —   —

One evening, several weeks after the pizza-flipping incident, Brennan was unwinding in the living room after finishing his homework, stretched out on the couch in front of his favorite TV show, *Just The 3 Of Us*, belting along with the theme song lyrics (as he liked to do when nobody else was around).

The series followed a struggling middle-class family of three, the *Aislingers*—a mom, a dad, and their mischievous-yet-good-hearted son—as they all navigated the daily challenges of school, work, parenting, and making ends meet. Brennan knew that the Aislingers weren't a *real* family—just a bunch of actors on a stage *pretending* to be a real family, with a studio audience trained to laugh on cue at their every goofy facial expression, or slapstick pratfall, or witty comeback—but in their general dilemmas and conflicts with each other, they reminded him of a nicer, happier, funnier version of his own family. And even though the main boy in the show, *Brian*, was a few years older than he was, the fact that he was confident, hilarious, and cool in all the same ways Brennan wanted to be—as well as their names sounding so close to each other's—filled him with the secret wish that *Just The 3 Of Us* was actually some kind of temporal magic-mirror, broadcasting a surreal vision of his future back through time, straight to his living room, just for him to laugh at and look forward to.

A few minutes into his show, he heard a vehicle pull up and park outside. When it was followed moments later by the slamming of a door, Brennan paused his show and listened until he heard the sounds of a man spitting curses to himself as loud as if he were cursing at someone else.

Oh, Daddy's home, Brennan thought, and clicked the episode back into motion.

The man outside had been simmering in his rage for the better part of his workday after learning during his lunch break—second-hand from a co-worker, no less—that he was passed over for the big promotion he had been counting on, in favor of his boss's nephew, who had only just started at the company.

He stomped up the concrete path that parted their front yard, bouncing the bag of their dinner against his thigh to the rapid rhythm of his steps, and still muttering curses under his breath, when something small tapped against his foot—no harder than a big raindrop— capturing his attention and stopping him in his tracks. He glanced down and saw a cluster of petals hovering above his foot, no bigger than a gumball, shimmering a pale, glow-in-the-dark green in the dim streetlight. It was a dandelion that had grown so tall, its massive head dragged the stem down into a long arch, creeping over the edge of their entrance path. He crouched down, briefly observing the arcing weed where it stood before plucking it and rising to his feet, examining it further up close.

He looked out across their yard, examining both sides, and noticed that their lawn had become noticeably overgrown compared to those of their neighbors. Not what he would call 'shabby', by any means, but... Not exactly *well-maintained* either, and the last thing the father wanted was for their neighbors to start talking. He already carried enough shame with him.

He sighed and tossed the weed out into the street, admitting to himself that he hadn't stayed on top of his yard work since the spring thaw... But his thoughts quickly shifted from exploring questions of why *he* hadn't mowed the lawn, to questions of why his *son* hasn't mowed the lawn, and the more he thought about it, the more a singular thought began to form and circulate in the father's mind: *I just can't think of one-good-reason why the boy can't start mowing the lawn.*

He has other chores, after all, the man thought to himself, *tidying his room, and helping his mother with the dishes and laundry... So, what I'd like to know is, why can't he ever seem to find time in his busy schedule to help me out with any of my chores once in a while? Lord knows I was mowing the lawn when I was his age... Is it really just too much for a father to ask his own son to help him mow the lawn these days? Too much to expect everyone to pull their own weight around here—to believe I deserve even a crumb of respect from my own family...?"*

Those were the kinds of thoughts whirling round and round the father's head as he entered the house, finding his son feet up and laid back in his usual evening spot, nestled up snug in the glow of his favorite TV family.

"Hey, daddy... How's work?" Brennan said, his voice distracted and dreamy, glancing sideways at the man before returning his gaze to the characters on screen.

"Yeah, hey... Ehh... Lemme ask you something... In your comings-and-goings lately, have you *noticed* the state of the yard out there, by any chance?"

The boy returned a confused expression, but he sat up quickly and paused the show. "The *what, huh...?* The... *Yard?*"

"Uh, yeah, the *yard*—you know, the great big green thing out there in front of the house? Practically up to my knees, just about. You stay real quiet and look out there long enough, you might just even spot Tarzan, or one of his other jungle-pals, swinging around from vine to vine."

It took Brennan a beat to make sense of his father's words, but once he did, he smirked and scoffed, then threw himself back against the sofa, cracking up in a giggle-fit and saying, "You're so funny, daddy!" before picking up the remote and unpausing the TV.

The father made a tight, sucked-in frown, nodding his head, and let out a loud sigh through his nose.

"*Mm.* Yeah. Okay. Well, as '*funny*' as you might think I am—you know what's really *not* funny to me? *Hm?*" He stomped over to his son, snatched the remote off the couch cushion and thumbed the TV off, then flung the device onto the coffee table where it landed with a jarring *clack.* "...Well, I'll go ahead and tell ya: it's how *disgustingly* dismal and overgrown we've let our front lawn become—because *I* don't think that's very funny at all! Do *you?*"

Brennan scooted himself back against the couch and sat up straight, shaking his head. "*Wha*—*no*, daddy. I... I don't think our *lawn* is funny at all—*really!* I *promise!* …It's just that, when you said—"

"Okay, so then, what? *Huh?* Do you just want our neighbors to think that the people who live here are all shameless, deadbeat *slobs?* That *I'm* a deadbeat? *Huh?* I mean, for crying-out-loud, son, why is it *so* hard for you to ever take any *pride* in the roof that your mother and I work *so hard* to keep over your head? Unless, *what,* you just think you're *too good* for yard work or something? Is that it?"

"I—*no*, daddy, that's not… I just… I'm *sorry*, daddy. I just thought you were joking before, about Tarzan and stuff… But I *do* like it here. In this house… I like it here a lot. And I know you and mommy work super hard… And I, um… I don't think I'm too good to do stuff… And I do still *water* the grass, sometimes… Like, not *every* week, but still every *other* week—just like I'm supposed to, right? Does that count?"

The father had actually forgotten about this chore of his, as he was usually at work when Brennan watered it, and for just a passing moment, the man found himself embarrassed and taken aback by his oversight.

But for some reason, something about having his own error offered back to him—and especially the meek, supplicating way in which his son offered it—only served to stoke the man's irritation further. He placed his hands on his hips and cocked his head to the side. "Ohh, okay, *wo-o-ow.* I guess I must've forgotten somehow that *big man* over here finally figured out how to turn on the sprinkler hose—well, *bravo!* Look, son, any idiot can *water* a lawn—but you're not just *any idiot.*" The man looked away and began pacing the room, rubbing his chin as though contemplating some deep thought. "No, at your age, I expect you to be out there, actually *mowing* the lawn and putting in the hard work—a little *elbow-grease,* y'know? Really building up a sweat and pulling your own weight around here for once. …And hey, you know what else? Going forward, it's not just gonna be *our* lawn, either. Yeah, no, from now on, you can go around, door-to-door, asking our neighbors if you can start doing *their* lawns, too. And yeah, sure, you might groan and grumble about it *now*, but it'll only help build up your character in the long-run—you'll see, you mark my words."

"O-okay, daddy. I'll do it," Brennan said, nodding in agreement through a confused squint, "I-I-I'll do the lawn mowing now, whenever you want. I will. And I'll do our neighbor's lawns, too, if that's what you want. Okay? But, I... I still don't really get why you're being all..." He paused, carefully considering his next words.

The father stopped pacing and turned to face his son, propping his hands back up against his hips and scowling, then raising his eyebrows in a gesture of sudden curiosity, before a mean smile darkened the man's face. "*Yes...?* Oh, no, please— continue. Go on. You were saying: *You don't get why I'm being all...* 'Being all' *what* though? What is it *exactly* that you think I am... '*Being all*', huh?"

"I-I'm sorry, daddy! I didn't—I didn't mean to—" the boy said, his mouth opening, closing, sputtering and sucking down air like a fish gasping on land, his brain a nonsense tangle of words and bad feelings.

"—Well, c'mon, what is it? You don't have to be '*sorry*'— just *tell* me. Spit it out already. What? Don't tell me you're afraid of your old man, are you, son?"

Brennan knew the man was not going to let this go, so he took a deep breath and gathered enough of his focus to remember his earlier thought. "No, I just—I was just going to say that, like... Well, I just don't really get why you're being so mad at me right now about the lawn. Like, it was never on my chore list... A-and you never told me anything about it or how to do it... And I didn't even know you *wanted* me to do it for you until, like, right now."

The father straightened, letting a deep chuckle out through his nose while still holding his glare. "*Are you—*" he groaned a sound through his nose that sounded equal parts laughter and growling, then cleared his throat before continuing, an uneasy calm steadying his voice, "Are you actually *sassing* me back right now?"

"Oh, *no!* No, daddy, I *wouldn't!* I-I just—I'm not trying to—"

"—Nah, you know what? You go ahead and be quiet now, boy. And I mean, *right now.* And there'll be no more of this *'daddy'* nonsense either. You're not some *goo-goo, ga-ga* little baby any more—despite whatever *your mother* may think—so I'd say it's finally time for you to stop talking like one. No son of *mine* is gonna be raised into some prissy little snowflake. Yeah, no, from now on, you can start referring to me as *'father'*—or better yet still, *'sir'*—a title that carries at least a *hint* of dignity and respect. *Oh...* And from now on—if it's alright with *you*—I will be the one who decides who *is* and *isn't* sassing me. Or disrespecting me. Or treating me like dirt. Or laughing at me behind my back, and stepping on me, and walking all over me like I'm not even standing *right here the whole time!*" He closed his eyes, took a deep breath, and set their dinner bag down on the coffee table, then he straightened and began fussing with the belt buckle of his pants. "No, you know what? I might have to take that kind of treatment *out there*—from *them*—but I will *not* be ridiculed or disrespected in my own home—and *certainly* not from my own son, I can tell you that right now. No, by God, you are going to learn some respect today, young man... And I'm gonna be the one to teach it to you... The same way my old man had to teach it to me." He dragged the leather belt free from his waist and folded it in half, gripping an end in each fist. He brought his hands together so the slack between them made a gap in the middle and jerked the two ends apart creating a whip-like *crack* that carried throughout the house, making the boy's whole body jerk and tense up as if a gunshot had unexpectedly gone off in front of his face.

"Oh, *no,* daddy—I, *err*—I mean, *father,* uh, *sir*—please, no—I didn't mean it—oh, *please!*"

But there was nothing the boy could do. His father had him within moments, and for the next while after, the boy's screams of pain and terror filled the house.

—   —   —   —   —

When his father had finished, he shoved the sobbing child aside onto the couch and rose to his feet, staggering a few steps away from the boy, all red-faced and sweaty. Between his breaths, he told him, "Now... You go on, get outta here... Off to bed... Disrespectful young men don't deserve to eat their dinners... Your leftovers'll still be there waiting for you, so you can eat 'em in the morning, before school... Now, go... And don't you forget to call me 'sir' from now on, or else we're gonna need to give you another little refresher course on *respect*—you *comprendé?*"

The trembling boy couldn't bring himself to look back up at his father, but to his father's shoes, he said, "Y-yes, s-sir."

"*Good.* Well, have a goodnight then. And sleep well."

But Brennan did not sleep well. The backs of his thighs, hips, waist, and bottom all hurt so bad from his father's belt, he had to lay on his stomach through the whole night. And even once he was finally able to drift off, he kept turning over in his sleep, lighting him up with pain and snapping him awake as though he'd just rolled over onto burning red coals.

But the next morning, still sore all over and half-asleep, he got himself up and ready for school as usual, reheated his kid's meal from the previous night's dinner, and set out once more on the long walk to school.

Brennan was never very invested in his parents' religion growing up, though he did enjoy attending Sunday morning church services with them alright enough.

He liked how, from the time they walked up within earshot of those church doors until the moment they sealed themselves back into the car for the drive home, his parents *had to* get along and act nice. And his church wasn't one of those old-timey churches with music provided by the pale and trembling hands of an ancient church organist, no, *his* church had a full rock band setup, complete with moving lights, high-definition, programmable displays, a smoke machine, and even a stage that whizzed and whirred apart, revealing a small pool underneath for baptism ceremonies. Brennan loved how the services gave him the chance to sing as loud as he wanted, without anybody ever looking at him funny. And he liked how the people who got up and talked on God's stage spoke about magic and supernatural powers, as though they were real and still happened all the time in our real world, if we can all just believe the right things and make God happy with our prayers. But Brennan could never understand why everyone who ever went to speak up there all had the same weird way of talking, their voices all going up real loud and then shrinking soft and quiet, sounding the whole time like they were talking about super-important stuff, even when they weren't. And he didn't get why everyone who ever got up to talk about those cool magical, mythical, ancient people and stories always made them sound either *boring*, or *corny*, or—worst of all—*scary*. He never laughed whenever they made their cringe jokes that seemed to crack up everyone else around him. And whenever Brennan found the nerve to ask why they spoke that way, there was always an adult nearby to either deflect or silence the question.

So, while he didn't exactly *mind* going to church with his parents on Sunday mornings, he never felt much of a personal inner-connection with the things they always wanted to talk about up on God's big, loud stage.

But on that morning after his father first belting, for nearly the first five minutes of his walk to school, he pressed his clasped knuckles between his eyebrows and he prayed as he walked—pausing and peeking an eye open after every few steps to ensure he wouldn't bump into anything or veer off into the street—asking God to please keep him from saying, or doing, or being anything bad ever again...

Or at the very least, for the rest of that day.

—   —   —   —   —

From that time on, Brennan stopped watching TV in the living room altogether, hoping to avoid risking his parents' wrath for doing some bad thing that he didn't even realize was *that* bad. Instead, after completing his homework, he would seclude himself in his bedroom, spending his time playing with his toy heroes, watching his TV or playing video games.

It was also around that same time that—without him even realizing it—Brennan started picking up a few nervous habits during his down time, while his mind was busy doing other things.

These weren't the kinds of habits he might try to build in order to take better care of himself—like drinking water, brushing his teeth, stretching, or getting more exercise—these habits were just fidgety little things that he would do with his hands, all the time—almost uncontrollably—without even thinking about them.

He never noticed when he started biting his fingernails, yet, over time, he picked and gnawed and pried at them whenever his hands were free, scaling them back until he could see, and *feel*, the angry pink skin beneath, stinging like papercuts where the nails joined the skin.

And while sitting at the edge of his bed, facing his screen, he would tap his dangling toes so hard, he would shake his entire bed without ever even feeling it.

It got so bad at school that the kids sitting nearby would sometimes have to nudge or poke him to get him to stop his finger- or toe-tapping.

Whenever Brennan heard one of his parents arriving home in the evening, he would listen and wait until he heard them go into the restroom, then he would slip silently out of his room and down the hall to the kitchen, to investigate the dinner situation. If dinner was a kid's meal burger or nuggets, or anything else that came in its own single-use wrapper, he could snatch his portion from the fridge and squirrel it away back to his room and eat his dinner by himself. If it was pizza, anything that came in a bowl, or anything that could otherwise make a mess, then he wasn't allowed to bring it back to his room, and would either have to wait until after his parents had gone to bed, or until the next morning to eat his food in peace.

Even when he could manage to avoid them, whenever both parents were home together late in the evenings, he could still hear them in the other rooms throughout the house, snapping, cursing, insulting, or otherwise bickering with each other all throughout the night until either he, or they, eventually fell asleep.

Yet, despite Brennan's best efforts to be a good boy every day, and even avoiding his parents entirely, it seemed that every other week or so, one of his parents would return home from work, slam the door, and call out across the house for their son. He would then leave his room to meet them, and there, they would explain to him whatever perceived misbehavior that they had taken offense to, which would, once again, require him to face a physical punishment.

With his mother, it was usually her pinches. With his father, it was usually his belt.

Neither parent ever noticed the link between their worst, most stressful or aggravating days at work and what they saw as their son's "bad" or "lazy" or "selfish" or "disrespectful" behavior; much like their *bills*, their *jobs*, their *bosses*, their *coworkers*, and most recently, their *spouses*, both parents now perceived their son's misbehavior as nothing more than the most recent woeful link in the endless chain of burdens and miseries that they had been cursed to endure, and only pitied themselves all the more for their lives.

And so it went for weeks, and then months, with the hours he spent at school serving as the boy's greatest respite from his daily worries about being a *bad boy...*

But that all was about to change once Brennan entered the fifth grade.

Four.

Before the start of his summer break, Brennan learned that his fifth-grade teacher was going to be a man—Mr. *Q-something*—which would mark the first time that Brennan had a *Mr*-teacher instead of a *Ms-* or a *Mrs*-teacher. He was thrilled for the change of pace and wondered how a male teacher might differ from his past female teachers; if this new one might be funnier and tell them more jokes, or if he'd still read them stories with silly voices for the different characters, or if he'd generally be more silly or more strict, overall. His head swam with curiosity, wondering just how many ways the fifth grade would set itself apart from the rest. He was so excited that, on the first day back to school, he even left his house an extra fifteen-minutes early that morning, just so he could be the first of his peers to pick out his seat before class started.

When he arrived at his classroom and selected his seat—one near the middle of the room, so he was never too far away from anything—he hadn't even noticed the shadowy figure sitting hunched over a desk in the darkened back corner of the room, quietly pecking away on his laptop.

"*Oh!* Hello, sir, and good morning! I didn't see you back there when I first came in, or I would have said *hello* sooner! My name is—"

The man raised his head just enough for the boy to see his eyes, illuminated and hovering just above his laptop screen, his brows bunched together into an irritated crinkle above his nose, then he waved Brennan off as though fanning away flies. "— *Young man*, class has not yet begun and I would very much like *quiet*, please. You see, I'm a quiet man, myself, and I very much enjoy quiet in my classroom. I do hope that won't be a problem for you—and, *more importantly*, I hope that *you* will not be a problem for *me*. Now, if you can bring yourself to curb these inane, primal urges to prattle on interminably, and instead, stay perfectly silent until I call on you, then you may remain in your seat. If, however, you are indeed some feral creature, utterly lacking in self-control, then you may instead go out and find yourself a seat on the hallway floor, and wait out there like a dog until the sound of the bell. Just know that, should you choose to remain where you are, my class does not begin for another 15 minutes, at which point, I will expect you to *remain* in silence throughout the course of our daily lessons together. Now, boy, *is that understood? Yes? Good. Thank you.*" Then the glowing eyes of his teacher ducked back down, vanishing once more behind his laptop screen.

Brennan was speechless. The man had said *please* and *thank you*—as nice, polite people always do—but there was something about the cold way the man responded to his warm greeting that gave the boy a heavy, aching feeling in his chest and stomach, as well as the sudden urge to cry. He folded his arms on his desk and rested his forehead on them as the minutes passed by, until, eventually, the rumble of children resonating throughout the outer hallways grew in volume and intensity. When the thunder of schoolyard friends all laughing and catching up finally started pouring into the classroom, Brennan dried his eyes on his sleeves, sat up straight, and waited quietly and attentively for the day's lesson to begin.

When the clock struck eight and the bell chimed throughout the school, the secluded figure in the dark corner snapped his laptop closed and rose from his desk, standing so tall, his head reached higher than the top of the chalkboard, casting an imposing figure in the dim light, like what Abraham Lincoln might have looked like if, instead of becoming the US president, he grew up to become a grizzled and cantankerous old prizefighter.

He grabbed a black cane that stood leaning against his desk, and with great limping strides, he stormed over to the center of the chalkboard that spanned the front wall of the classroom. He tossed the cane upward in front of him and caught it in the air by its midsection, then rapped its large silver grip five hard times against the blackboard—*THACK-THACK-THACK-THACK-*

THACK—and belted the word, "*QUIET!*" as loud as a military drill instructor. The whole squawking, laughing, chittering chatter of nearly three dozen children instantly dropped into complete silence. The man stood facing the class with a hard, pitiless glare, his hands clasped over the grip of his cane, rocking up and down on his heels as he surveyed and scrutinized the fresh young faces of this new batch of students. If any of them looked at his face closely, they would see him subtly shaking his head and frowning as his disapproving gaze drifted from one child to the next.

Once he had concluded his survey, he pivoted on his cane, spun back around to face the board and snatched up a piece of chalk, then, pinching the white stick by its side to write in thick, wide lines—visible even from the back of the classroom—he drew a big circle on the board followed by a slash through its bottom-right corner.

"Now, *that*—" He gave the blackboard another hard *THACK*, then spun back around to face the class. "—for those of you geniuses who *still* don't know your *ABCs*—is the letter *Q*, and *that* is the first letter of my name. And since I don't have all day to waste listening to you little pea-brains stutter and stumble, trying to pronounce a five-syllable name, then—should the occasion ever rise that you have an adequate reason for speaking to me—you may refer to me as '*Mr. Q*'—and I will even accept, '*Mr. Quiet,*' if it helps you remember. But let's all just do what we can to avoid ever speaking to each other directly, and hope that it never comes to that, *yes...?*

"Now, as *that young man* already learned earlier," he said, pointing to Brennan in his seat, "I enjoy quiet in my classroom. So, when you arrive in this class—*any* of you—I expect you to be... *Quiet*. There is nothing of any significance that any of you have to express to each other here, in this classroom, that you cannot share during your designated break times, and I *sincerely* doubt that there is anything—no matter how trivial—that I could possibly stand to gain from hearing what any of *you* have to say. Therefore, I will expect you all to remain as quiet as you are right now throughout the course of your daily lessons with me. *Understood? Great. Good. Thank you.*"

—   —   —   —   —

Brennan did his best to listen, stay focused, and take in the day's lesson, as always, but Mr. Q's intense demeanor of sternness-bordering-on-anger made him feel nervous, like he could say or do something bad without a moment's notice—and the man's habit of whacking his cane against the blackboard did nothing to help settle the boy's already frazzled nerves. He never looked away from, or focused his attention on anything aside from, the teacher right in front of him, but for some reason, whenever Mr. Q spoke, Brennan felt like he was standing in the middle of a busy freeway with cars and trucks whipping by him, one after another, each one close enough to touch. His head rang with the tone of a panicked voice, beating like a pulse within him, saying, "Don't be *bad*... Be a *good* boy... Don't get in *trouble*... Be a *good* boy..." over and over, on the same endless loop that played through his head every evening when he would freeze, hearing the sound of keys in the doorknob, keeping an anxious ear out for just how loudly his parents closed the door behind them.

Times like these, Brennan felt like he almost couldn't understand words anymore—or had somehow forgotten what they all meant—and struggled to put them all together into any sensical shape or meaningful order. He kept catching his wandering attention every time the teacher cracked his cane against the board to emphasize a point—and each time, the boy would jump in his seat with no recollection of his last few minutes, as though he were suddenly startled awake, even though he had been staring at the man the whole time.

Throughout the lesson, he kept tapping his finger on the top of his desk and tapping his toe on the floor beneath it. His fingernails were already chewed down to swollen red nubs, but he quickly discovered that the side of his pencil served as a fine substitute for his urge to gnaw.

—　　　—　　　—　　　—　　　—

Once Mr. Q had completed his morning lecture, he told the class to write an impromptu essay on "*The Virtues of Silence*". Neither the boy nor any of his classmates had any idea what they were expected to write, but none of them wanted to risk provoking the wrath of their hulking teacher by being so bold as to speak to him out-of-turn.

So, just as he would have done any other day at school: he thought hard about what the teacher had asked him for, then he would work to complete the assignment to the best of his ability—and his first step would be to teach himself what the word, "*virtue,*" meant. So he rose from his seat and made his way to the reading corner in the back of the classroom, where he pulled a dictionary from the bookshelf, but as he headed back to his seat, he saw Mr. Q glaring up at him over the top of his laptop screen and he froze where he stood.

"You there, *boy*," Mr. Q said, "Tell me, what could have possibly possessed you to relieve yourself from the work I assigned you and take a leisurely stroll around my classroom?"

"Oh. I'm sorry, sir. I didn't want to bug you by talking to you or asking you any questions, but, well, I needed a dictionary. So, I just got up to, uh... To, um... I got up to, uh..." The boy felt his whole body shaking, like his legs could give out beneath him at any moment.

"—'*To get a dictionary*'—*yes, yes!*" Mr. Q rolled his eyes and huffed, shaking his head. "But tell me, dear dough-headed child, are you able to *raise your hand* without speaking?"

"Uh, yes, sir. I can do that."

"*Excellent!*" He said, stressing the word in a mock-congratulatory sing-song. "In that case, the next time you find it necessary to leave your seat, you can simply raise your hand and wait until I feel like calling on you. Once I call on you, *then* you may move about, *silently*, and if you do anything that I don't like—anything at all—I will be sure to let you know." He smirked a cheesy, sarcastic smile, holding it for all of one second, before his expression fell slack and he ducked back down behind his computer screen.

"Um… Thank you, sir."

Mr Quiet's arm extended out from behind the screen and shooed him away with another dismissive wave of his hand.

The boy returned to his seat and flipped through the dictionary until he found the entry for *virtue*—"*noun: moral excellence; goodness; righteousness*"—and would have needed to look up some of the other words, but he was certain he knew what *goodness* meant, so he set about writing down everything he could think of that was good about silence.

After they'd been writing for some time, Mr. Quiet closed his laptop, stood and yawned, stretching his hands up high over his head and then bringing them back down to scratch his ribs. He picked up his cane, hobbled around to the front of his desk, and stood leaning against it for a moment, observing the students hard at work, before rising once more and beginning a slow walk around the classroom, weaving a serpentine path between the rows of desks.

The boy was so engrossed in his writing, he didn't even notice when Mr. Q was standing right behind him—not until the ornate silver handle of his cane came cracking down on his desk, ringing through the classroom like a gunshot. Up close, Brennan could see that the jagged, swirling shapes on the handle was the shiny sculpted image of a great white shark, bursting up through the surface and suspended mid-leap in the air, surrounded by a great splash of silvery waves.

Brennan leaped in his seat, his whole body tensing up like his teacher had just dumped a bucket of ice water on his head.

"*GAH*—sorry, sir! Di-did I do something wrong, sir?"

"*Wrong*, you ask? Hmm. Well, I suppose that depends... You see, I was drawn to the little impromptu percussion recital you decided to put on for us all." The boy looked confused, so Mr. Q slowly crouched next to his desk, groaning like a bear the whole way down, and began drumming his thick fingers against the side of the boy's desk, saying, "*Tapita-tapita-tap-tap, tapita-tapita-tap,*" before abruptly ceasing his drumming fingers and glaring silently down at the boy as he rose, gradually, back to standing.

"Oh, I'm very sorry, sir! I think I do that sometimes and don't even know I'm doing it, but I promise, sir, I will try really hard to—"

"—*If* you'd be so kind, *boy*, please, refresh my memory... Did I, at some point, *ask* you to provide us with any musical accompaniment for today's writing session?"

"Well, uh, no, sir, but—"

"—And did I announce to the class that I enjoy *music?* Is *that* what I said I enjoy?"

"W-well, no, sir. What you said before was that you—"

"—Ah, yes—*now* I remember... I said that I enjoy *quiet!* Now, tell me, boy... Were you exhibiting *quiet* just now?"

"I, uh... I, um..." Brennan was already panting in short, rabbit breaths. He could hear the thumping of his own heartbeat, feel it pounding away in his chest and his temples. He couldn't speak or think of anything to say in his own defense, but he also had a feeling that his teacher—like his father—would only get more and more angry with him the longer it took him to reply. So, he dropped his head, looking down at his still-tapping toe and forcing it to stop, and he said the only two words he could manage: "...No, sir."

"Mm. *No, sir,* indeed. Even though you already assured me once today that you would not be a problem. Regardless..." He saw the boy's notebook lying open, flat on his desk and snatched it up like a falcon swooping in to capture its prey. "Let's see what you've managed to write on the subject of *silence*—a concept you seem either uncomfortable or unfamiliar with…"

While the teacher cleared his throat, the boy sunk his head down between his shoulders and placed both of his hands on the top of his head while Mr. Q read what he wrote out loud to the class.

"*I like silence. I like quiet. And I think that* 'thay'—misspelled—*are good. When it's quiet, my body feels good. When it's quiet, my brain works good*—improper grammar. *When it's quiet, I don't feel like crying and I am not so scarred when it's quiet*—simply *terrible* sentence structure here—just *shameful*, really—and I *believe* you meant to write the word, "*scared*" here, not "*scarred*"; we have *got* to work on your spelling, boy… Moving along… *I don't feel so bad when it's quiet. There's no yelling when it's quiet. When it's quiet, I don't have to worry about my mommy or my… Father being mad at me—Ha!* It looks like you scribbled out the word '*daddy*' here and wrote '*father*' next to it—such crude fixes might have worked in prior classes, but to me, this looks as revolting on the page as a big hairy wart, and I will not accept such crude sloppiness from your pages again going forward. Now let's see here… *Cause when they get mad, they yell at me, and then my head hurts and my heart hurts and I just feel so scared, it feels like I'm gonna die from being so scarred*—I find it so curious how you managed to spell the word '*scared*' correctly the first time here, then went back to the double-r for the the second… …*and I really don't want to die*—well, you don't *say?* As none of us particularly *wish* to die, it's a rather redundant thought to express in writing, *don't you think?*—though, I suppose, no more redundant than anything else you've managed to put down here… Alright, final stretch, let's see… *I love when it's quiet and I just get to be me and I don't have to worry about being a bad boy. But as much as I love when it's quiet, I love my mommy and father even more. And I know that, even though they get mad at me a lot, they love me back.*"

Mr. Q made a loud, whistling sigh, and dramatically wiped his shirt sleeve against his forehead, as though he had just completed a hard day of heavy labor, then tossed the notebook back onto the boy's desk where it skidded to a stop.

"Now then," said Mr. Q, rotating in place to address the class, "let this be a lesson to all of you; this chicken-scratch *drivel* that I just read aloud for you all is to be regarded as our standard for the lowest possible expression of your thoughts that I will even *consider* accepting. If, going forward, any of you submit another work to me that is as poorly written as *this*—or heaven-forbid, somehow *worse*—then I will tear your paper into confetti in front of you and demand you start over, rewriting the entire thing again and again, as many times as necessary until it is acceptable—now, *is that understood? Yes? Good. Thank you...* And as for *you*, boy..." He spun back around, looking down at Brennan, placing his heavy hand atop the boy's head, and tussling his hair. "You shall stay after school today and rewrite this paper until I find it free of errors."

Then the man hobbled back to his desk and remained there until the end of the day, when he passed out the students' homework for that night: a century-old, 200-page novella about an old fisherman that would be the focus of their writings and discussion for the next day.

—   —   —   —   —

After all the rest of his classmates had gone home for the day, Brennan found himself having to write and rewrite his paper on *The Virtues of Silence* a total of four times—including the first draft, which Mr. Q had read out loud to the class—before he was finally allowed to pack up his things and head out into the dark on his long walk home.

—   —   —   —   —

Once at home, he started on his chores first—since he didn't want his parents to come home before he had finished them, and he didn't know exactly how long his homework would take (since he had never been expected to read an entire book in a single night before). Even though he was hungry, he knew that one of his parents would be showing up with dinner before too long, so, rather than spoil his appetite with his usual noodle cup, he decided to pick up his reading for the night's homework and wait for his dinner to arrive instead.

When his mom came in, her hands crowded with big bags of their evening meals, she saw her son reading at the kitchen table. "Oh, *wow!* First day back and you're already hitting the books hard, huh?" Then, while hanging up her coat and slipping off her shoes, she playfully asked him, "*So...?* How was our big fifth-grader's first day back-to-school?"

Brennan turned his head from the book, just long enough to say, "Mm... It was fine, I guess," then returned to his reading.

"What—that's *it?* Just *fine?*" His mother laughed. "Come on, it *had* to be better than that, right? Tell me about it! Did you learn anything new? Make any new friends? What's your new teacher like? Is he *fun?*"

Brennan sniffed and said, "*Meh...* Not really..." Then he marked his page, set the book down on the table, and proceeded to tell his mother the sad story of his miserable day.

Once he had finished filling her in on everything leading up to her walking through the door, he was left with a hollow, scraped-out feeling aching in his chest from having to relive all of those painful and embarrassing moments over again.

Whenever these types of *'serious'* moments came up in *Just The 3 Of Us*—the quiet, vulnerable parts of the episode, when the live studio audience falls library silent—when the Aislinger family breaks down and shares their innermost pains or fears or feelings with each other, the family would always come together in embrace, empathizing with what the suffering family member— usually *Brian*, the son—was going through, and once they were all feeling good again, and the studio audience was laughing again, they'd work together to figure out a way they might improve the situation.

And if, in those moments, his mother would have only reached out and pulled him into her, enveloping him tight in her warm comfort and nuzzling her cheek against his hair, telling him how awful and embarrassing that all must have felt, or how sorry she was that Mr. Q spoke to him in such a callous and hurtful way, or that she would speak to his teacher about a more reasonable homework load—as well as demanding that he treat his students with more dignity and respect—then Brennan would have burst into a puddle of complex and cathartic tears, and the scraped-out aching inside of him would have begun mending and healing itself on the spot, as if by magic.

But, instead, his mother just raised a curled finger-knuckle to her lips while she thought, then she cleared her throat into it and said, "*Wow*... That sounds like... *Quite* a day. I mean... Your father and I weren't exactly expecting you to come home with news that you were crowned *student-of-the-day* or anything, but... To hear that you *kept* getting yourself into trouble, over and over, on just your *first day*—and with your *new teacher*, no less... Well... I'm just very disappointed and sorry to hear it. And I'm sure your *father* will be, too. You're just lucky *I'm* the one who found out first; this way, you'll get away with just a few little pinches, rather than your father's belt again. Oh, and I don't want you touching this burger I got you—*or* leaving that table and sneaking off to your room—until *after* you've finished all your homework for tonight. *Capiche?*" She stood facing him, arms folded and legs apart, while her son just stared at her with wide unblinking eyes as the noise in his brain grew louder and louder. "Uhh, *hello-o-o? Earth-to-kiddo...?* I'm asking you a *question*; I *said*, '*Do you... Capiche?*' You *answer me* when I'm talking to you!"

"*Oh!* Uh, *yes*, mommy—*sorry*," Brennan said, his attention snapping him out of his thoughts and back to the conversation, "I just—I was just thinking about how much reading I still have before I'm, uh... Anyway, yeah, I understand what you said before. You're saying: 'No doing anything until I finish my homework,' right?"

"*Good.* Now... Come on, get over here... Arms out—*both arms*, come on, come on... Let's get this over with..."

—   —   —   —   —

An hour or so later, when his father came home, Brennan called over to him, without looking away from his book, saying, "Hi, father-sir. I'm just trying to stay up until I finish my homework, then I'll go to bed." But when no reply came, he turned from his book to see the man, and found his father looking nothing short of miserable; his arms slung limp and lifeless at his sides, and his slowly shaking head drooped down so low, his chin rested against his chest. "Uhh... Is everything *okay*, father-sir?"

His father raised his shoulders and sucked in a deep breath, letting out a dramatic sigh so loud, the boy could read the *particular tone* of the sigh even from the dining room. "No, son... I wish it was, but I'm afraid everything is *not* okay... Your mother texted me a little while ago and told me *all* about your first day back-to-school... How you kept misbehaving, slacking off, not listening in class, talking back, and just generally getting on your new teacher's 'bad side'. I mean, don't you remember what I always tell you about how, 'you never get a *second-chance* to make a good *first-impression*'? Well, it looks like you're about to learn that lesson the hard way... Gosh, you know, I'm just... We're *both*—your mother and I—just so, *so* disappointed in you, son. I mean, *seriously*—what were you even *thinking?* And on your *first day?* What, were you just trying to show-off in front of the other kids or something? Give 'em a little class-clown routine?"

"Well, I—"

"—*Stop,*" the father said, making a pained face and waving an open hand between them, while his other hand massaged his forehead, "*Just...* Stop. I don't want to hear it, son. And there's no use trying to lie to me about it either—you'll only dig your hole deeper and make things worse on yourself."

"*Oh*—But-but, *no*—but, father-sir, I wasn't going to *lie* to—"

"—*Quiet!*" The father shouted the word as loud as a drill-instructor, then he closed his eyes and held out his hands, palms facing his son, recognizing that he was getting dangerously close to losing his patience with the boy. He huffed his frustration out of his nose, and continued speaking with his eyes closed in slow, deliberate calmness. "Now… Your mother mentioned to me in her text that she had already punished you for today, so *hopefully*, that will be enough for you to learn your lesson."

The boy looked down at his arms, running his eyes over all the blotchy, aching lumps and mounds, the tiny, curved little cuts where her acrylic nails dug in hard enough to break and tear the skin. "*Yeah*…" the boy said, "I sure *hope* so."

"Me too, son… Me, too." The father headed to the kitchen, where he plated and reheated his dinner in silence. Once he was finished, he carried his food and drink back toward their bedroom, halting himself after a couple steps into the hallway and turning to call back to his son, "…And you do remember your mother telling you, 'No dinner 'til *after* you've finished your homework,' right?'

"Yes, father-sir," the boy called out in reply, closing the book around his page-holding finger to check his progress and saw that, thus far, he had only managed to read through the first *quarter* of the book. "*No dinner*… I remember."

"There's a good man," his father said. "Now, you hurry up and finish your work here, and get a good night's sleep, and tomorrow, I trust that you will make a greater effort to be a good boy and do as you're told."

"Yes, sir. I will. Er… Goodnight."

And with that, the father disappeared into his room for the night and the boy returned to his assigned reading, feeling even sadder and more ashamed than when he first got home from school.

Five.

The next morning, Brennan awoke, hunched over and aching. The sides of his head pulsed and pounded like a car alarm was going off inside his head. His cheek and the corner of his mouth were stuck to a small puddle of drool that had soaked into the page he was reading—as well as several pages behind it—when he eventually passed out. His eyelids were stiff, so dry and encrusted with sleep residue, they scraped his eyes as he blinked them open, gradually reacquainting himself with his surroundings.

It took him another moment still to recognize that the annoying, repetitive droning sound he was hearing was not coming from inside his own head, but was, in fact, blaring from a distant room and—in a snap—his whole body tensed and jerked suddenly upright, as if he'd just been shocked back to life by some mad scientist, springing out of his chair, stumbling through the kitchen and down the hallway as fast as he could. Once he made it back to his bedroom, each shrill blast of his morning alarm felt like its own sharp little pinch to his brain.

When he smacked the *off* button, he heard his mother's croaking voice yell out from their room, "*UGH—thank you...*" followed by a quieter, "*...Finally.*"

The boy studied the face of his clock as his eyes continued adjusting, trying to run the mental figures needed to figure out just how long he had overslept. After a minute or so of staring blankly at the numbers on its face, he'd determined that he was running about a half-hour behind his usual schedule, which meant that, if he wanted to make it to school on time, he would have to head out the door in... Five minutes.

As he didn't end up making it as far as undressing himself for bed the night before, he was, fortunately, still wearing all the same clothes from the previous day—a little dirtier and smellier, *true*, but at least that would save him a handful of minutes. He could skip showering and brushing his teeth, as well—*just for this one day*, he thought—and that would also save him some time. But then he felt his stomach rumble and had to stop and think. He did feel *very* hungry, as he had not eaten anything at all since his noodle-breakfast the previous morning. He glanced back up at the clock face and saw that two minutes had already passed while he stood there, figuring out what to do.

He sprinted back down the hallway and around to the kitchen table, packed his book away in his school bag, snatched a styrofoam noodle-pack out of the cupboard, filled it with water, and set it to nuke for two-and-a-half minutes in the microwave. By the time it finished, he figured he should have just enough time to grab his noodles, stick a fork in them, and run out the front door. And when the microwave sounded its first beep, Brennan flung its door open and did exactly that.

He had barely made it out to the sidewalk past the end of his yard, when he stopped to try the first sip of his breakfast, realizing in a panic that the broth in his mouth, the still-blocky noodles in his cup, and—more and more so—the styrofoam cup he was holding them in, were all still scalding hot. He was so hasty in his hunger and his urgency to leave the house on time that he had forgotten how—while it only takes two-and-a-half minutes to *heat* his breakfast—they still required several minutes out on the counter to let them cook and cool down enough to eat. Brennan's eyes bulged and he spat the hot broth out onto the street, moaning, *Eaugh, eaugh, eaugh-h-h-h*, to himself as he fanned tiny, ineffective puffs of air against his tongue with his fork-holding hand.

He still had a few more minutes before the noodles would be ready, so, careful not to spill the piping hot broth sloshing around the cup's rim, he brought the noodles up to his eye-level with both hands as he stepped down off the curb—one hand supporting its base, the other, curved around its lip and side—and set about carrying it across the street as slowly and carefully as a tight-rope walker.

The boy had only managed one more step when a loud engine, revving and roaring somewhere off in the distance to his side, captured his attention. He stopped, turned to look, and spotted a red sports car speeding up the road toward him. Judging from how far away it was, the boy was certain he had enough time to make it the rest of the way across without any trouble—but he did also have to walk slower than usual because of his sensitive cargo. And it didn't help matters that his school bag—packed so tight with all of his big new fifth-grade books that it was hard to zip closed—was now disproportionately heavy to the boy's size, weight, and strength, adding an otherworldly heft and chunkiness to each of his steps, like he was wearing a deep-sea diving suit. Still, he kept a close eye on the orange broth-level sloshing around the rim of his cup. He couldn't afford to stop and turn his head again, but with the oncoming scream of the engine growing louder and more intense with every passing second, the boy figured he should pick up his steps even more, splashing the burning broth all down around his fingers in the process, panting in pained bursts of, *Ah-ah-ah-ah-ah...!*

It seemed that every way he adjusted his grip, whichever hand carried most of its weight, he couldn't find any way to carry the thing without burning himself more and more with each step toward the curb—while also remaining careful and determined not to drop it.

At last, his front foot connected the opposite curb, mid-step, and he was traveling with such speed and momentum that he nearly flew face-first onto the concrete, but his rear foot sprung forward, catching him at the last moment, and then the other foot, until he was able to catch and stabilize himself without much further spilling or burning. The boy paused there for a moment and caught his breath, smiling to himself. He stirred his fork around the noodles and saw that they had softened, so he twirled a big round wad of them onto his fork, blew on it a few times, opened his mouth wide and—

—HO-O-O-O-O-O-ONK!

The red car blurred by him with such a blast of engine thunder, it would have been understandable for any unsuspecting pedestrian to have been shaken by the sudden loud noise—but coupled with the unexpected blaring of the car's horn right as it zipped past, the noise startled Brennan enough to make his cup-holding hand suddenly leap, tossing his entire cup of hot, brothy noodles up into the air where it came splashing back down, all down the front of his clothes.

The red car slammed on its brakes, skidding a few feet and creating a cloud of nostril-burning black smoke from its rear tires.

Brennan, still in shock, turned to look and saw the head and chest of a young man in a baseball cap—a highschooler, perhaps—rise up out of the red car's sunroof. He cupped his hands around his mouth while the driver revved the engine, and shouted just loud enough for Brennan to hear, "*Sucks to be you, dude!*" before ducking back into the car and tearing off down the road.

Brennan sighed and ate the bite on his fork, then stuck the fork in his pocket. While he chewed, he pulled the bottom of his shirt out in front of him so he could see just how bad the mess looked—his mind noisy with all of the things he imagined the kids at school might say—then he glanced down at his watch, and let out another defeated sigh, nodding his head in agreement.

Yeah... he thought to himself, sniffing back quick little breaths through his nose, as he tried to quiet the painful noise in his head and in his heart enough to figure out what he was going to do next. *Yeah, I guess it kinda does.*

—　　　—　　　—　　　—　　　—

By the time Brennan arrived at school, the soupy mess all over his clothes had mostly dried, leaving just a crusty orange stain behind. The rapid tapping of his sprinting footsteps echoed throughout the empty hallway as he rounded the corner into his class, where he found his teacher, already standing before the classroom, delivering his lesson, before stopping mid-sentence and holding his open hand out to the boy.

"Oh, no. No, no, no, no, *no*... No, I'm afraid not," Mr. Q said, shaking a finger in his direction without turning to face him. "No, if there's one thing I enjoy more than *quiet*, it's *punctuality*. Go now. *Shoo.* You may wait outside in the hallway until I am good and ready to indulge your tardiness."

Brennan checked his watch and it was true; he was indeed five minutes late. Later than he had ever shown up to a class before.

He made himself a space on the cold tile floor of the hallway and waited there, weeping every once in a while as he spent his time reading more of his unfinished book from the night before. As Mr. Q never came out to collect him, he remained out there, reading throughout his entire first breaktime, as well as the entire following class period, but when the bell rang for lunch and he only had one page remaining in his book, he got up, waited for all of the other students to exit, and knocked on the classroom door, asking his teacher if he could go to the lunchroom to eat.

Mr. Q only glanced up at him for a split-second, scowling, and waved the boy away. "Boy, why would you think that *I* would give two figs about what you do or don't do on your lunchbrea—" then he did a double-take, looking back up at Brennan and remembering him as *the tardy little cretin who disturbed the morning's lesson.* "Oh. It's *you.* I had completely forgotten you were *here*—marked you *absent* for the day. Mm, no matter, I suppose... Tell me, boy, just how late *was* it that you came *storming* into my classroom like some raging anarchist, *hmm?*"

"Oh, it was, uh... Five minutes, sir."

"*Oh, was it now? Was it five minutes, really?*" he said in a snotty, nasally sing-song, then raising a sharp eyebrow at the boy, continued. "Well, if *you* say it's five, then it was probably more like *ten*—so I'll just go ahead and mark it down as ten, and be *grateful* I don't mark it *fifteen*, just for this inconvenience... *Oh,* and did you happen to complete the homework I assigned?"

The boy beamed at the question, remembering that—at long last—he only had one more page left to read, and still smiling, with his back straight and his head held high, he said, "Oh, well, *technically*, no, sir, but I only have one page left, and I can just read that one right now on my—"

"—*Ah, yes*... Of *course*..." Mr. Q said, shaking his head and smiling at some thought that amused himself, "I suppose I really *should* have assumed that somebody like *you*, with no regard for himself or anyone else around him, would be woefully negligent in your studies as well—it's my own mistake for assuming the best in you, really—though, I suppose, I shall consider *this* my *lesson-learned*. As for *you*, however... Well, I'm afraid you'll find no easy-street short-cuts in *my* classroom, young man."

"Err... *No*, sir," Brennan said, only catching vague glimpses of what his teacher was telling him.

Mr. Q squinted his eyes at the boy, jutting out his jaw and wagging his tongue like a pendulum along his bottom row of teeth, a little lump darting back and forth beneath his bottom lip while he sat rubbing his chin, deciding the boy's fate for the day. "*Right then*," he eventually said, clapping his hands together loud to emphasize the word, '*right*'. "You are to stay behind for two-hours after class today and finish the remainder of your homework—whichever comes *last*. Is that understood?"

"Wait, but, *sir*—*!*" the boy said, instantly sick to his stomach at having to voice his objection, "—I mean, *can I ask*, sir, why I have to stay behind for two whole hours? I only have one page of last night's homework left to read—and I'm sure that one page won't take me a whole *two hours* to get through."

"You misunderstand me, boy—as is, I suppose, to be *expected* of your ilk," Mr. Q muttered under his breath, "But the two hours is your *punishment* for not finishing your homework, *and* for being ten minutes late to my classroom. You see, if a student of mine disrespects me by showing up late to my lesson— thereby, wasting *my* time—then I shall punish them, in turn, by taking their time back, *tenfold*. So, since you were ten minutes late, I figure ten-minutes-times-tenfold equals... *One hundred* minutes—not that I would expect a little empty-headed know- nothing like *you* to *know* or even *remember* this very *basic* and *common* fact, but there it is, nevertheless. But a *hundred minutes* is only *really* '*one hour and forty* minutes', and '*a-hundred-and-forty-minutes*' *hardly* sounds as good of a punishment as 'two-hours', now does it? It just feels *clunky* and *awkward* to me—not as *clean* as 'two hours'. *Oh.* And while you may only be one page away from finishing *yesterday's* reading, you are still well behind the rest of the class when it comes to writing the book report I expect on my desk first thing tomorrow morning. Now, please, go, and let me enjoy the rest of this brief reprieve from the unpleasant sight of ignorant young faces."

The boy nodded and left the room without a sound, first walking, then gradually picking up speed until he was jogging, and then sprinting, down the hallway to the cafeteria. When he reached the lunchroom, hardly any students remained, except for a handful of kids painting a large banner for some upcoming school event. He navigated his way around their workspace, careful not to disturb any of their crafting materials, and had only managed to reach the lunch service line when the bell sounded, beckoning him back to class.

Brennan sighed, sniffed, buried his hands in his pockets, and headed back to his classroom, with his stomach biting and growling at him in protest the entire walk back.

—   —   —   —   —

The book report ended up taking Brennan *three* hours to complete after school that day, and even though his hunger made him feel very weak and sleepy, he forced himself to run as much of the way home as he could, knowing that the previous night's dinner was still waiting for him in the fridge.

So, when he got home, he ran back to his room to throw his school bag onto his bed, then back to the kitchen, where he grabbed his leftover burger from the fridge, popped it in the microwave, and before it even had a chance to cool down, he had devoured the entire thing in eight ravenous chomps—and while he didn't get much of a chance to taste it, since it was there and gone so fast, he felt certain it must have been the most satisfying burger he had ever eaten.

He had barely managed to gulp down his last bite, when his father entered, holding a pizza box braced between his hand and his shoulder. "*So?*" he asked, "How was our big fifth-grader's *second* day—hopefully, better than the *first*, right?"

"Oh, yes, sir!" The boy said, wiping his mouth with the edge of his hand. "Much, *much* better than yesterday! I was able to finish up all of my homework for today while I was still at school—my first-ever book report!"

"Aw, that's *great*, son! I'm glad to hear it! And you didn't do anything to get on your teacher's bad side?"

Suddenly, the boy felt quite dizzy, and the burger that tasted so wonderful only minutes ago had turned sour in his stomach, and he could no longer breathe as slowly or as easily as he had before his father asked him that question. "Uh, well," the boy said, his eyes scanning the floor between them for nothing in particular as he tried to put together a good response, "I... *Tried* to be a good boy..."

The father set the pizza box down on the arm of the couch, sighed, drooped his head, and buried his face in his hand, rubbing his eyes with his thumb and finger. "O-*kay... Here* it comes..."

"No, *really!* I tried so hard, but I spilled hot noodle stuff on myself and that made me late to class, so I had to wait in the hallway like a dog, and then when I told him I didn't finish last night's homework—"

The father's head jerked upright, his eyes immediately fierce. "—Wait, you didn't even *finish* your—are you *kidding me?!* After *everything* we told you yesterday, you *still* decided *not* to finish your homework?!"

"I mean, I didn't *decide* not to do it—I fell asleep while I was reading and then—"

"—*Oh*, I see... You went to *sleep*..." His father stood, legs wide apart and fingers digging into his hips, nodding his down-turned head as he drilled his tongue into the soft flesh of his cheek, then his head swung up, revealing a face that was creased and strained tight with anger, his voice explosive. "...Even when we *explicitly told you*: *no dinner* and *no sleeping* until you finished your homework! Oh—and let me guess, you ate your burger in there, too?"

"Well... I mean, yes, I ate the burger, but not *last ni—*"

"Oh my God—*stop*... Just, stop. I just... I don't want to hear it anymore, boy..." The father unbuckled his belt with a metallic *cli-click* sound, like he was loading a tiny gun, then dragged it out from his belt loops. "I just can't tell you how disappointed I am in you, son... Or how much I wish we didn't have to keep doing this little dance."

"*But—no! Please! No, father-sir!* Please, *no!* I *promise* I'll be a good boy again, sir! I *promise!*"

"Now, you *quit* all that bellyaching, right now. You get over here and you face your punishment like a man... And no more lies, *huh?* I mean it. You're only ever digging yourself in deeper. Now, obviously, your mother's *light touch* with you last night wasn't enough to leave any kind of impression, so—*once again*—it looks like your dear-old-dad's gotta step up and be the *bad guy* again. Believe me, boy, this isn't any more fun for me than it is for you... Now, you get over here... I'm not asking you again..."

Six.

And so it went for the rest of the week—as well as the week that followed—with the boy accidentally stumbling into some kind trouble with Mr. Q, which would then get him into trouble at home. But at the start of his third week in that classroom, something happened that would forever shape the course of Brennan's path in life.

When the bell rang that morning, Mr. Q rose from his desk and limped to the head of the class, as he did every morning, but before he spoke, he held a hand over his eyes and scanned the faces in the room. "*Right*, well, before we get started on today's lesson, we have some—*debatably*—important business to address... *New-kid?* Where's the New-kid? *Ah*, there you are! Come on, *come on*—get up here—we haven't got all day!"

Brennan turned back in his seat and saw a short, dark-haired boy—*noticeably* shorter than any of the other boys in their grade—standing at his desk in the back corner of the room, still holding up his hand, but he quickly dropped it and jogged up to meet their teacher.

"So, *class*, this is the new-kid; *new-kid*," he said, gesturing with a wave of his arm toward the onlooking students, "these are your classmates. So, *apparently*, class, this young man is, by *some* metric, marginally more intelligent than the lot of you—not that the bar is set particularly *high* in that regard—but his so-called '*gifted*' intelligence was enough to let him skip the fourth grade entirely. Whether or not he'll have what it takes to make it in *my* classroom... I suppose only time will tell... Now, while I'm sure many of you would like to skip our lesson for the day so we can waste our time asking this new-kid what his *favorite dinosaurs* are, or, *how he spent his summer vacation*—but *that* is not why we're here today. No, by God, we are here to *learn*, and so far, we've already—look at this, I can't believe it—we've already wasted over *two minutes* of our precious learning time on these,

these... *Social trivialities...* No, absolutely not, if any of you want to get to know your most recent classroom cohort, then you can jolly-well do so during your own designated break times—now, is that understood? *Yes? Good. Thank you—*and *you!*" he said, sneering and pointing a finger down in the new kid's face, "What in *blazes* are *you* still doing up here? Get back to your seat, child! *Now! Go!*"

Once the new kid was back in his seat, Mr. Q loudly cleared his throat and proceeded to deliver his morning lecture.

—   —   —   —   —

While Brennan had spent much of the previous couple weeks staying late after school—an hour here, a few hours there—he was, by no means, the *only* student in class to have drawn Mr. Q's punitive brand of irritation.

It seemed that every time he was told to stay late, he was joined by more and more of his fellow classmates. One girl asked to take a restroom break twice in one day, and, upon returning from her second trip, she learned that she'd had to stay after-class for two hours—"*That's* one hour *for each time you wastefully abused your class-time*," explained Mr Q. Another time, a kid returned from lunch while still licking his fingers and chomping away on his last mouthful of food, and that alone was enough for that boy to lose his lunch-break privileges for an entire month. Then, there was another girl who Mr. Q made an example of when he caught her *humming* to herself during their writing time; he brought her before the class, declaring her to be a dangerous anarchist in need of severe reeducation, and that any further *humming*—or any other non-verbal vocalizations—were to be considered, '*intolerable acts of willful insubordination*'. He kept that girl so late after school, that, by the time she was finally allowed to go home, the night custodian had to unlock the school door to let her out.

It was during some of these after-school punishments, as well as throughout their breaks and lunchtimes, that Brennan managed to form a friendly connection with a handful of his classmates who knew just how harsh Mr. Q's methods could be.

So, after Mr. Q's morning lesson was over and the class poured out of the room for their first break, Brennan headed outside to meet up with his usual group of schoolyard friends, and he found them—along with a crowd of many other kids from other classrooms, both younger and older—all gathered in front of the new kid under the shade of the big sycamore tree atop the hilly corner of the yard, and already flooding him with questions, like, *Where are you from?* and *What kinda stuff d'you like?* and *How were you able to skip a whole* grade*?*

The new kid found some of their questions funny, and giggled sweetly before answering,

"Well, my family and I, we just moved out here from the east coast, after my mom got sick," and, "I like all *kinds* of stuff! On weekends, my dad teaches me martial arts—which is kinda like karate and stuff—so I'm really into that right now. But I also really like books and movies, music, games, TV—prety much everything!" and, "I guess I don't really know *why* I skipped a grade. Not really. I mean, my education is super important to my parents—and to me, too, I guess—so they try to teach me stuff in the best ways that I can learn, and... I guess that just helped me learn a lotta stuff pretty quickly. I was homeschooled before, but when I signed up to go here, I had to take a test to get into the fourth grade—reading, writing, and math stuff. Then, a couple days later, they called my parents, telling them I had to come back and take another test. After that *second* test, they called up again, telling my parents that I'd be starting in the *fifth* grade instead... And, well... *Here* I am."

Even though it was only his first day at this new school, there was something undeniably magnetic about this new kid, with nearly everybody who met him instantly wanting to talk and hang out and be friends with him. He had an adorably round, cherubic face, but more than that, there was some quality in his eyes—particularly, the way he very slightly closed them every time he smiled or laughed—that gave him the appearance he was always smiling, even when he wasn't.

Whenever something struck him as *unusual* or *uncomfortable*—like that morning, when Mr. Q presented him to the class without even the courtesy of introducing him by *name*, only to then rush him back to his seat—he tried to recognize whether the issue was with himself, or with somebody else. He had already been taught, and understood, that it is not always possible to avoid unhappy or discourteous people in life, and knowing that fact, he knew better than to take his new teacher's rudeness personally—though he *did* have a good little *inward* laugh, seeing a fully grown adult act in such a silly and undignified way, with all the patience and maturity of somebody *much* younger than anyone else in their classroom. This new kid was often able to laugh off such minor irritations, and generally didn't let very much get him down. He was unusually self-assured and secure for someone his age—carrying himself with an air of humble, measured confidence that some people seek their whole lives and never find for themselves—but he also didn't take himself so seriously that he couldn't laugh at his own mistakes, or even a tasteful joke at his own expense—as long as the joke was actually *funny*.

Brennan spotted another kid who arrived late to their break-time gathering—a tall, gangly boy with greasy black hair that draped down past his nose, saying, "*Sorry... Sorry... Sorry...*" to those around him, meekly weaving his way through the openings in the crowd. Then, once he was close enough to see the new kid clearly, he called out his question from the crowd's edge in a cracking, hesitant voice, asking, "So, uhh... What kinda stuff do *your* parents hit you with?"

The other children standing around the kid with the long black hair all turned to see who had asked—surprised, at first, by the boldness of his question, then gradually nodding at each other and muttering amongst themselves in agreement that it was a pretty good question.

The new kid was visibly taken aback by the startling bluntness of what he *thought* the boy with the long black hair had just asked him, almost certain that he had misheard the question somehow.

"Uhh, I'm sorry... I don't think I heard you right... Could you come a little closer, please?"

The crowd between them parted and the tall kid made his way through. Once he made it close enough that his head could be seen clearly over the heads of his shorter classmates, the new kid sucked down a quiet gasp at what he saw. The black-haired boy's entire right eye-socket was filled in with various shades of blotchy reds and purples, fading back into fleshtones near the highest corner of his cheek, and his right eyelid swollen half-shut. He removed his own tight grip on his elbow long enough to wave an awkward, flailing, *Hi,* before grabbing it again, then he ducked his head down, and flicked his eyes between the grass at his feet and the new kid standing in front of him. "I, uhh—oh, *hey, new kid! Welcome!* ...I just, uhh... Well, I was just asking—I mean, my *question* was: *What do your parents hit you with? — And it's fine if it aint nothing but an open hand;* that's pretty normal, I think—but I was just wondering if they *hit you* or *beat you* in some *different,* or, like... *Special* kinda way that helped make you so super smart or something. That's all. I was just wondering."

The new kid's mouth drew low and tight with concern at the question, and he only grew more concerned when he saw how many undisturbed, curious faces all stared back at him, eagerly awaiting his answer.

"*Look*... I know you're *new* here, new kid," chimed one girl near the front of the crowd, "but you really don't need to be shy or embarrassed. Trust us: *e-e-everybody's* parents hit them with *something* when they're bad—even if it's just a regular ol' slap-upside-the-head for saying some dumb thing you ought-not-to."

"—Well, *my parents* send me to the apple tree out back, so's I can pick out the stick they's to swat me with!" blurted one boy in a t-shirt and denim overalls with long coppery hair that was short in the front and sides, but flowed long and shiny down the back of his neck, then his eyes popped open with some sudden discovery and he started waving his hands around at the others. "Oh, *he-e-ey!* That *rhymes,* what I just said! Wait—let me try that one again real quick!" Then he cleared his throat and started again, closing his eyes and holding up his finger, as though he were performing a poetry recital. "*I must go out and pick... The stick they'll beat me with... And it* better *not be too dang small! ...'Cause if it's just a twig, and they find one that's* big..." Then the boy paused a moment, squinting his eyes and tapping his finger in the air to the tempo of the rhyming scheme in his mind, bobbing his head to the rhythm, and mouthing the preceding words a few times before finally opening his eyes and concluding, "...*Then they'll swat 'til I'm achin' and raw!*"

The kids within earshot all cracked up at his morbid little verse—even Brennan, who could have sworn he had never heard such good rhyming in his life—but the rhyming kid shook his head and raised his arms once more, quieting them all back down.

"—*No, no! Wait!* I got an even *better* one!" He cleared his throat again, then proceeded, "...'Cause if it's just a twig, and they find one that's big... *Then they'll swat 'til I can't walk at all!*"

The children all burst into even harder laughter at this revised line—with a couple of them even exchanging knowing glances and nodding along in recognition—all except for the young new boy, who just looked on with an expression that was now bordering on *horror*, until one of the kids shook him out of his thoughts, asking him, "So... How 'bout it, *new kid?* We told you about *us*... So whadda *your* parents hit you with?"

The new kid could have never expected to be asked such a shocking question—at least, not without it being some kind of strange joke at his expense. But this was no joke. Neither the boy with the long red hair, nor any of the other quiet, onlooking faces, revealed any trace of humor—if anything, their expressions were the opposite of *knowing humor*. Their faces were all stretched long with open-mouthed curiosity, leaning in, craning their necks, and holding their breath, while they waited for the new kid's answer.

If it weren't for the anxious chewing of his bottom lip, the black-haired boy would've looked completely frozen in time, gripped in a trance by this genius-new-kid-who-miraculously-skipped-a-whole-grade, as though this kid was some great guru or ancient master, who might somehow deliver him from his own suffering circumstances, while also teaching him a better way to live—and all through some profound nugget of life-wisdom about the *best* method for a parent to beat their child.

The new kid hesitated, stammering a moment before he could reply. "Well... I mean, *nothing!* My parents would never use *anything* to '*hit me with*,' don't be *silly!*" but he immediately felt bad about adding the '*don't be silly*' part at the end, hoping it didn't come across as *mean* or *rude.*

"Oh... Okay. Cool-cool-cool..." said the black-haired boy who had first asked the question, nodding his head in comprehension. "So, just, like... *The plain open-hand,* then—got it... Yeah, that's nothing to be ashamed of. Kinda wish *mine* would just use their open hands and nothing else. My dad doesn't need to use anything, 'cause just his hands are bad enough—I mean, *obviously*," he laughed, gesturing up at his dark, swollen eye-socket, "but my mom always does more damage with her big ol' *chanklas,* or those little belts of hers, or—*God forbid*—one of the cooking pans, than she *ever* does with just her hand by itself. Anyway, you should be glad you only get their *hand,* kid."

"*My mom* uses a wooden spoon on me!" one girl's voice blurted out, "but I'm actually *lucky* that's all she uses, because *her mom* used something called a '*phone cord*' on her back when *she* was bad—which, I guess was like some kind of charging cable or something from *olden-times*—but anyways, she said that it hurt her just as bad as a *real* whip!"

"Well, my dad never really *hits* me anymore," said another kid with fuzzy hair clipped so short, Brennan could see all the skin underneath, "but whenever I'm bad, he usually just takes my favorite stuff out front to the driveway and runs over it with his truck... You know, like, toys and games, souvenirs and trophies, that kinda stuff—which, I guess, sometimes, I kinda wish he would just hit me around a little bit instead, because then, like, I'd still have those things and they wouldn't all be gone *forever*... But it's all whatever, I guess." Then he shrugged, sniffed, slumped his head, and stepped back into the crowd.

A hush rippled throughout the crowd after the last boy's testimony, with many in the crowd drooping their heads and sagging their faces, a few of them even closing their eyes, as they imagined a variety of scenarios in which their own parents would be angry enough to destroy their favorite toys, keepsakes, or awards as a means of psychological or emotional punishment. Watching their little nightmare scenes play out so vividly in their minds—as well as the countless different ways each of those scenes could play out—an air of sadness made its way through the crowd, swelling up in the heats of all who had heard what the boy with the fuzzy short hair had to say; a heavy, aching feeling, filling up their chests like dense, dark fog and pushing their hearts deep down into their guts—as though the bitter and painful scenarios they'd dreamed up had all actually happened to them.

While most of the crowd remained head-slumped and ruminating on their sad thoughts, Brennan stood off to the side, psyching himself up to share his own experience with home discipline. From his position, he could only see the left side of the new kid's face in profile, so when he wasn't initially called on, after finally gathering the nerve to speak up and raising his hand, he leaned over, stretching himself across a few people in the front row and waving his outstretched hand in a blur.

The new kid spotted Brennan waving in his periphery, sighed, and muttered to himself, *I sure hope* you *have something happier to say*, and the moment their eyes met, Brennan slid the rest of himself through the crowd to the front.

"Hey, so, like, I never told anybody this before," Brennan said, speaking faster than usual, "but, like… Well, I guess my dad can hit me pretty bad sometimes with his belt—I mean, it's not like he breaks my bones or anything, but it hurts so bad after, I just… I feel like… I mean, like, I *know* it's supposed to hurt pretty bad and everything, so I can really learn my lesson, but I just think that, like… Maybe it's not supposed to hurt *as* bad as it does? Or for as *long* as it does? And what if, like, maybe he doesn't actually *know* how bad it really hurts, but then if I tell him, he'll get mad at me because he'll think I'm being disrespectful. And he always gets maddest at me when I'm being disrespectful... But it's fine, probably. He hardly ever has to do the belt thing. That's only ever for when I'm extra, *extra* bad. Usually my mom just gives me these hard little pinches all up and down my arms."

Brennan thrust his arms out for all to see, and the kids huddled around him all stared down at them, studying the residual blemishes his mother's pinches had left behind.

"It looks like you were attacked by a chicken or something!" One girl called out, cackling.

"Oh, yeah, I guess so... Like, they always *hurt*, but sometimes—when she's extra mad at me for something—she'll dig her fingernails in and leave all these little slices everywhere that scab up and turn into these little white lines that won't go away. I just call them my little '*moon marks*'... You know... 'Cause they look like a bunch of little moons." Then he paused for a moment, realizing that he had never actually voiced his name for them out loud to anyone else before, but something about sharing made him feel good, like showing them his arms and actually talking about his pinches made it all feel more *real* for him somehow. He smiled and nodded his head, shrugged, and said, "...But anyways, I guess that's not *too* bad compared to some of you guys," before withdrawing himself back into the crowd.

The new kid was so stunned, he hadn't even realized that his arms and legs were trembling. No words came to his mind. He just blinked and blinked, shaking his head in disbelief and knitting his brow into an uncharacteristic face of confusion-bordering-on-frustration, and sputtering little gasps as he gathered the words and sounds to form his response. "*Wha—I...* Well, *no, that's not what I—I didn't—I just...*" then he stopped himself, closed his eyes, took in and let out a deep breath, collecting himself before continuing, "...*Okay*, so, what I *meant to say* was, my parents *don't* hit me. At *all*. Not with *anything*. Not their *hand*, and not with anything *else*. No spankings. No slaps-upside-the-head. Nothing. They just *don't hit me*. Like, *at all*. They never have. They just don't believe in it." When no response came, the new kid punctuated his statement with a slow shrug of his shoulders and an apologetic frown.

Then, as if on cue, the school bell rang, announcing that break-time was over and it was time to return to their classes, but not one foot stirred in the whole crowd. Their faces, somehow, looked even more awed and captivated than before. The new kid darted his eyes about the crowd, waiting for someone—*anyone*—to break and turn back toward the school, but when nobody did, he cleared his throat, saying, "Uh, *well*, thanks for coming and hanging out everybody... It was great to meet you guys, but... I should probably be going now, and start heading back to—"

"—*Ay-O! New kid!*" snapped a stocky young lady from the back of the crowd, sporting a pair of tight, dirty blonde pigtails and a sour, puggish expression fixed on her face. She stomped her way from the back of the crowd to the front, never breaking her pace, clearing her path with a few effortless shoves and swipes at the kids in front of her, knocking them down—and into each other—like a pig-tailed bowling ball careening down a lane full of lanky little pins, creating enough of a disturbance that the remaining kids in her path all scrambled to clear the way on their own.

Once she had made her way through the crowd and cleared the front row, she kept storming up toward the new kid without slowing her stride, looking like was on her way to punch him in the face. The new kid had to step—and then momentarily, *stumble*—backward to avoid getting trampled by this 6th-grade-juggernaut, but when she reached him, she halted with regimental stiffness, squaring up to the young boy whose head only came up to her armpits, and standing so close, he had to tilt his head all the way back just to look her in the eyes.

"You're coming back here at lunch time, new kid," she said, greeting him with a couple of sharp, two-fingered pokes down into his chest, making him wince with each little jab, then she raised her poking fingers close to his face, "'Cause, *if* what you say is true—and that's a big *if*, as far as *I'm* concerned—then I think me and some of these other *fine people* here are gonna have a few more questions for ya—questions we're gonna want *answered.*" She punctuated her last word with a final jab into the chest, making it as clear to him as she could—with the limited communication skills that she had—that her invitation to '*return at lunch,*' was *not* a request, and she was *not* asking.

By that point, most of the crowd had already dispersed and wandered back into the school, and the ones who remained—including Brennan—all nodded their heads in agreement with the stocky girl, before retreating to their classes as well.

The new kid held his hands up to the big girl, nodding his head quickly, while looking down and away from her, in a display of, '*I'm afraid,*' and '*Please, I don't want any trouble,*' and '*I'll do whatever you want, just don't hurt me,*' without saying or doing anything that might cause her to feel threatened—just as his father had trained him to. "Oh... Uh, yeah, sure! I can come back here at lunchtime. Happy to answer any other questions you guys got."

"*Good.* That's good..." the big girl said out of the raised corner of her sneer, dropping her hand onto his shoulder and adding a couple of firm pats before leaving it resting there—his entire shoulder joint enclosed in her palm, with her thumb running the length of his collarbone—and using it to lean her weight against him. Her hand felt so large and heavy to the new kid, he thought it felt like she was wearing a baseball glove, but the new kid did not move to react, confident that the interaction would conclude at any moment. "I guess you *are* pretty smart, after all."

Satisfied that she got what she wanted, the big girl with the pigtails removed her hand by way of dragging it down the side of the boy's shoulder, like she had something gross stuck to her hand and was wiping it off on his shirt. Then she scoffed, blowing air through her teeth, and finally, she turned and strolled back to the school.

Once the new kid felt she was a good enough distance away, he scooped up his backpack and sprinted back toward Mr. Q's classroom.

The new kid wasn't necessarily *afraid* of the big girl with the pigtails, but she also didn't seem like someone whose '*bad side*' he wanted to be on, either. So when the lunch bell rang, the new kid sprung from his seat, snatched his lunch bag out from his cubby, and raced out of the room, down the hallway, outside through the double-doors, and up the hill toward the tree in the high corner of the yard.

When he finally made it, he hunched over, resting one hand against the tree's trunk and the other on his thigh, his heartbeat thundering in his head and his chest heaving with short, ragged breaths that scraped the little boy's dry throat and filled his lungs with ice. While catching his breath, he glanced back down the hill and found that, aside from a small handful of kids only then starting to trickle out of the various school exits, he was the first to make it outside for lunch.

Maybe some of them are still grabbing their food in the cafeteria, he figured.

Relieved to be the first one there—and especially to have made it there before the pigtailed girl—he set his things down and took a cross-legged seat on the grass. He snapped his lunch kit open and snacked away on his compartment of mixed berries while watching the busy scene develop below him. His schoolmates skipped and lept through the air, spreading out like ants toward the jungle gym and the sports field. Once he had picked his berry compartment clean, he packed the rest of his lunch away, closed his eyes, and focused his attention on his breathing.

After a few minutes, he heard the chatter and footsteps of a few other kids approaching, and then hushing their voices and shushing each other, before whispering their speculative chatter amongst themselves. Soon after, he felt the impact of a shoe's toe thumping against his knee. He blinked his eyes open, squinting up at the pigtailed silhouette towering above him with her arms folded across her chest.

There were somehow even more kids gathered around him now than there were during their earlier break, anxiously peeling away at their tangerines and string cheeses while they waited for the new kid to speak.

"*Oh*, good—you're here!" The new kid sprung to his feet, briskly rubbing any remaining grass off the back of his trousers, and saw how many others were gathered. "*Wow!* I guess you're *all* here."

The tall girl raised an eyebrow at him. "Wasn't sure you'd show, new kid. It's a good thing you did. Good for *you*, I mean…"

"Well, I said that I would, didn't I?" The new kid crossed his arms and shrugged. "And when I say I'll do something, I do my best to stay true to my word."

The tall girl scoffed, smirking and shaking her head at him this time instead of rolling her eyes and scowling as she had before when he said something she found corny. "Yeah, okay. Take it easy there, li'l boy scout."

He giggled at her remark. "Okay, well, you mentioned earlier that you had some questions you wanted to ask me?" Then he swiveled his head, looking from side to side, addressing the rest of his peers. "And I suppose some of you might have questions as well?"

The crowd erupted into noise at the prompt, their overlapping voices all drowning each other out into a droning, mind-splitting buzz, like watching a dozen TVs all blaring at once.

The new kid closed his eyes and took a deep breath before responding to his peers. "Okay, so I see that a lot of you still have some questions for me, but if we could please just try to stick to one question at a time, I will try my best to listen to all of you."

One kid raised her hand, and when the new kid raised his hand to point to her, the pigtailed girl side-stepped right in front of her, saying, "'Kay, so, before, right, when you said that your parents, '*don't believe*' in beatdowns, or whatever… Did you mean that, like, they don't believe that kids actually get *beat—*

because I *know* we do, and if that's what they think, then they must be pretty stupid because—"

"—Erm... *No*, sorry," interjected the new kid, holding up a finger, "that was *not* what I was trying to say. I think they probably know that there are a lot of kids out there who get hit. And I know that, too. They just don't believe that hitting *me* will make me behave any better or listen to them any better. For my parents, the idea of hitting their kid just isn't normal—it's *weird*."

The crowd gathered around him all responded in comprehending unison with an, "*Ohh...*" the chorus of their voices together all sounding like, "*Awe...*"

The pigtailed girl nodded her head, squinting her eyes and puckering her lips as she considered the kid's response. She felt a tap on her shoulder and turned to find the girl she'd stepped in front of glaring up at her. The big girl let her face fall slack into a closed-mouth deadpan, and she responded with a deep, nasal grunt that sounded like, "*Mm,*" and stepped aside, nudging and shoving those around her to make room.

With the pigtailed girl out of her way, the smaller girl raised her hand once more. It was the same girl from their earlier break whose mommy hit her with wooden spoons, and whose own mother was whipped with telephone cords growing up. When the new kid called on her, she picked her words slowly and gently, careful not to say the wrong thing; approaching her question with an anthropologist's spirit of sincere, scientific curiosity, saying, "So, wait... I still don't get it... Like, if they don't *hit* you, then... I mean, how do they *punish* you when you're bad or naughty or... You know... *Sinful...?* Do they just, like... Yell mean stuff at you until you feel sad?" Her eyes remained trained on her hands and their gestures for the entire time she was speaking, then once she finished, she looked up at the boy.

"Uhh... Well," said the new kid, having to pause once more to gather his reply, "I guess I would say that... Even the times when I mess up... My parents never really think of me as being 'bad'—or, I should say, at least not any more than they think of *themselves* as 'bad' or 'naughty' or, uh... *'Sinful,'* whenever *they* get cranky or scared or make mistakes. They know they're not perfect, and they know my heart. They know that I'm a good boy, and that I *want* to do good in the world, because I care about what it *means* to do good and to be kind and to help others when we see that they can use our help. So, I try to do my best, every day, but I still mess up sometimes. Like, a *lot* of the time. And whenever I do, they are kind with me, and they make time to sit down with me, and we all work together to figure out the problem and learn from the mistake. They know that I love them more than anything, and that I want to help them and make them proud, always. And I do always feel like they're proud of me, and that they love me and care about me. They think it's really important to teach me to be able to really *feel* my feelings, and how to talk about my thoughts and my emotions when I can, and they both have to do the same thing. Sometimes, they might talk alone with each other about different adult problems they have, but usually, if something is making either of them sad, we all make time to sit down and talk about it together, while the others listen calmly, with no interrupting allowed. That way, me, my mommy, and my daddy can all work together to make sure we all feel *seen* and *heard* and *cared for* by the other two."

One of the kids in the group scoffed, saying quietly to his friends—but still loud enough for the new kid to hear him, "*Pish-h-h!* Like, okay, *bet*, but peep how baby-Einstein here straight juked that punishment *Q* like some OP-ninja. Full cap, this kid, straight up—but he's a *rizzler* for real!"

The new kid craned his head back, crinkling his eyebrows at the strange remarks he didn't fully understand, but he continued with his best response to what he *thought* he was being asked, saying, "...Well, uh... As for how they '*punish*' me when I make a mistake or do the wrong thing... I know it might sound kinda weird to you guys, but... They don't really believe in *punishment* either. They told me before how punishments just make us *afraid*, more than anything, and how all that fear makes our growing brains all jumbled and confused until we can't think right or feel right, and—like they say all the time—*if we don't* feel *right, it's very hard for us to* act *right.*'

Everything Brennan was hearing from this new kid made a lot of sense to him—he *did* feel like his brain got all tied up in knots whenever he got scared—but he struggled to see how it all lined up with what his parents had taught him about punishments, and why they were so necessary. He tried arranging his thoughts into a single question he could ask, but too many of them competed for the top spot in his mind, and he couldn't bring himself to pick between them, but he raised his hand anyway, while no one else was talking, and waited for the new kid to call on him.

"Yeah, so I actually have a *couple* questions to ask, if that's cool?" Brennan said.

"Um, sure, yeah—I mean, as long as no one else minds. Hey, wait, you're in my class, right? You were here before... With the, uh... '*Arm pinches*'...?"

"Yeah, uh-huh—Brennan, *hey*. So, like... My parents don't really hit me *all the time*, right? But whenever they *do*, it's because they have to teach me some important life-lesson about stuff like, 'how to *respect* better,' or how 'actions-have-consequences,' and all that kinda stuff. So, like... If you never get hit or pinched or punished or anything, then, like... How do you ever learn your life-lessons?"

"Hmm... Well... I guess I already understand that my thoughtless words or actions can come with their own bad consequences. Like the time I tried to feel the sharpness of my dad's samurai ninja sword and accidentally cut my thumb open; I tried to hide the cut from my parents because I felt embarrassed and scared that they would be mad at me for doing something I knew I wasn't supposed to, but when they found me and saw how scared I was—crying like a baby with all that thumb-blood dribbling down my elbow, with a line of red dots following me all around the house—a mess that *I* would have to be the one to clean up later... Well, they felt that the cut itself and the consequences worked as its own kinda learning lesson. And I *sure* understood after that why he didn't want me messing around with his sword."

"Uh-huh... Okay... But, then, like... How were you smart enough to understand all of this weird stuff they were teaching you when you were still little—I mean, 'little-*er*'?"

The new kid laughed and said, "Well, they didn't really *explain* any of this stuff to me when I was little—they just *did* it. They never tried explaining any of these things to me until I was old enough to ask questions. But I also think that, when we're little, we can probably get used to just about *anything*—good stuff *or* bad stuff..." He paused, distracted for a moment by some visibly unhappy thought, then he lit back up, saying, "*Oh!* And they also taught me this thing called 'mindfulness'—which, I think they even talk about in *Star Wars*—but it's this thing that helps me stop whatever I'm doing and... Well, I guess I don't really know how to talk about it, exactly... My parents are *way* better at explaining all this than I am, but... I guess it's basically, like, just closing my eyes and focusing my attention on my breathing and how my body feels for a couple minutes, and also noticing the kinds of thoughts that pop into my head automatically, without me even having to think about them— kind of like looking up at the clouds and *noticing* what they look like, but remembering not to get worried if I see a cloud that looks like a scary wolf or something. It all just helps me slow down and think better. The *real* word for it is '*meditating*'—if any of you guys ever wanna try it with me sometime—but, in my house, we just call them '*breathing breaks*'. I would be happy to spend part of our lunch or break time doing a breathing break with any of you guys, if you want. I know that just sitting-with-your-eyes-closed probably looks like it would be *super* boring, but after you get into it for a couple of tries, it's *totally not!*"

"Uhh, *sure*, thanks..." Brennan said, scratching the back of his head and unsure of exactly where to look or how to respond to the new kid's boring offer to sit around and do nothing, "Maybe *some* time, but, like... I don't know..." Then he backed himself into the crowd, disappearing among the faces of his similarly unconvinced peers.

The new kid's bright smile dimmed a little as he scanned the crowd and saw that not one of the other children in the crowd seemed to share any enthusiasm—or even *interest*—in joining him. They shrugged, shifting their glances between one another, mumbling their non-committal replies, like, "Yeah, I don't know..." and, "Nah, I'm good on *that*," and even one, "I don't think I'm *allowed* to," while several others in the crowd simply dispersed and drifted off back down the hill toward the field or jungle gym.

The new kid held his hands up to them and laughed, saying, "Hey, no presh, guys! I'm just letting you know about it so that, if you see me sitting somewhere out here with my eyes closed, there's no need to worry—*that's* what I'm doing. Just a *breathing space*. And if any of you guys—or anybody else—ever wants to sit with me, you totally can."

As much of the crowd continued to dwindle, a taller boy with dull blonde hair who'd been standing next to Brennan throughout the lunchtime gathering suddenly uncrossed his arms and stepped forward, saying, "Yeah, I got a question for ya, smart guy..." His hair was a choppy, lopsided bowl-cut that looked like he tried to cut it himself, and the shaved back and sides of his head visible underneath his blonde mop gave it the appearance of being a wig.

Much like the pigtailed girl earlier, the blonde boy stormed up to the front of the group, close enough for the new kid to smell his lunch as he breathed down on him, and could even see its scattered remains strung like lumpy, brown garlands along his gum-line.

Beef jerky, the new kid thought. *Teriyaki flavored.*

There was something concerning about this blonde kid's demeanor that immediately set the new kid on his guard—much more so than the pigtailed girl earlier. He stepped his right foot back to stabilize his stance and kept his hands open and loose in front of him, just in case he needed to defend himself.

The taller boy twisted his mouth into an unflattering sneer and folded his arms across his chest, saying, "Yeah, you know what *I* think? I think this is all *bull. Everybody* gets hit. It's *normal.* So what? Get *over* it. Like, do you really think anybody here wants to turn into some cringe little crybaby-wimp? My dad *su-u-ucks,* but I'd still rather take my licks at home than turn into some woke li'l snowflake-turd like *you!"*

Then the blonde boy snorted back hard, turning his sneer even uglier as he rolled his head back, then flung it forward, launching a gooey yellow gob at the patch of grass right between the new kid's shoes.

The glob hadn't even had a moment to soak into the ground when, in a blur, the pigtailed girl was suddenly standing between the two boys, shoving the blonde kid back in the process, sending him flailing and reeling for several steps before ultimately tripping and stumbling backward onto the grass. He quickly rolled himself onto his side and sprung back up like an acrobat, smirking as he backed away from the crowd and holding up his hands in a gesture of mock-surrender, before saying, " *Whoa, easy there,* mountain-girl! Take it easy... I was already leaving..." then he leaned to one side, looking past her to the new kid, waving at him, adding, "Welcome to *real* school—" and ending his so-called welcome with one of the ugliest, most hateful names you can call a boy, before slinking off back down the hill.

At that, the bell rang throughout the schoolyard and the few remaining kids all drifted apart, making their way back to their classes, whispering their thoughts and theories about this new kid's strange story with each other.

The new kid overheard one of them saying to another, "Man, can you *believe* that kid?! What a little *liar!"* to which his friend replied, "I know, right? Like, if he can't even tell *us* how they hit him—and he has to make up all that weird stuff and *lie* about it like this—then he must get it *super bad* in *his* house! The poor kid's prolly scarred for *life...*"

The new kid was hurt by their comments in a way that he hadn't expected. He wasn't so upset by the blond boy's rude name-calling, or even sad that some of them thought he was a liar—though, that *did* make him sad, because he prided himself in his honesty—but more so by the casual ways these other kids all saw their abuses as a simple fact-of-life. He knew, as an abstract concept, that some kids' parents would hit and yell at them, but he had no idea how bad it could get, let alone that the kids themselves could ever come to view such treatment as a *good* or *normal* thing. It all felt like more sadness than the young boy's heart could take.

On his way back, he made a brief detour to the boy's room, where he wept quietly in a toilet stall. Then, after a few moments of calm breathing, he dried his eyes and returned to Mr. Q's classroom.

Seven.

The new kid's words echoed throughout Brennan's head for the rest of that day, making it harder than usual to focus on his schoolwork, but he managed to make it through the rest of his school day without getting into any trouble with Mr. Q.

When he got home that evening, he skipped his usual after school snack, raced through his homework, then grabbed three plates and napkins, and set three places around the dining room table. Once he finished, he remained sitting there, waiting for his parents to return home.

His mother was the first to arrive, setting her pizza box down on the couch arm and turning to close the door behind her. When she turned her back, Brennan greeted her with an enthusiastic, "Hi, mommy!" startling her so bad, she jerked, accidentally closing the door much harder than she had meant to, which then startled the boy in return, tensing his face and shoulders, and setting his teeth to grinding.

"*Ohmygod*—you startled me, kiddo! I wasn't expecting you to be right there when I came in. Feel like I haven't even seen you in *weeks*..." She eyed the well-lit dining room and the places her son had set around the table, as she loosened her scarf, hanging it and her purse on a coat rack. "Whoa, what's all this for? Don't tell me you're thinking of joining us for dinner and eating together like an actual *family*, or something?"

"Yeah, uh-huh! Does it look good?"

"I mean, yeah, it all looks great, but I just..." She picked up the pizza box and carried it across the living room toward him, sighing and staring up at the ceiling until she was standing right in front of him, then continued, speaking softly. "I really hope that this isn't you trying to *smooth something over*—you know what I mean? I just hope this isn't all to soften us up for some new trouble you managed to get yourself into. Because if so... I don't think it's gonna work, sweetie. You're... You're *not* in any new trouble, are you? ...Oh God, please, tell me it's nothing too bad, because I have so many things going on right now, I just can't deal with anything—"

"Oh, no, no, mommy! You don't need to worry about that. I'm not in any trouble."

The mother squinted her eyes down at him, then pursed her lips and sighed, setting the pizza box down on the dining table. "So, you're telling me that... If I called up *Mr. Q* and asked him how you were in class today, he would say that you were a model student, a good listener in class, and stayed focused on your work all day?"

Brennan shrugged. "I mean... He probably wouldn't say all *that*, but he'd say that I didn't get into any trouble. I was good all day—I swear. But this isn't about that."

"*Oka-a-a-y...*" the mother said, unable to shake the suspicion in her voice.

"It's just... I just kinda wanted to talk to you and... And my *father-sir*... About this kinda weird thing that happened at school today."

"Oh?" she raised an eyebrow, lifting the cardboard cover by its tab and splitting her focus between the food and the boy, "Wait—like, weird, *how?* I mean, like, what kind of weird are we talking about here?" She then dropped the pizza cover, turning to face the boy with wide, anxious eyes verging on panic. "Like, should I be sitting down for this, or—oh *God*, I hope it's nothing *too* bad this time, because I really just *can't* deal with this right now—actually, you know what?—just hold that thought a minute, I'm gonna go and pour myself a quick drink for this one—have a feeling I'm gonna need it... But you go ahead, sweetie... You keep talking, I'm still listening..."

"But..." the boy called back over the sounds of cupboards creaking and thumping, "Shouldn't we wait for... My *father-sir* to get back first?"

"Nah, you go right ahead, sweetie… We can fill him in when he gets here… And besides, it shouldn't be too long until he gets back." The mother returned from the kitchen with a soda can in one hand and a fat glass full of transparent orange liquid in the other. "Until then, I am all ears, and we can dig in!"

In his head, Brennan had planned on telling them both about his unusual day over dinner at the same time, but the pizza *did* look very good, and he felt so hungry, he couldn't even remember the last time he ate, as he skipped his lunch to hear what the new kid had to say. But it would probably be okay, he figured, to tell them about the new kid one at a time.

The mother had already grabbed her slices and was holding the cardboard lid open for her son. "Now, don't tell me you went and spoiled your appetite before dinner?"

He dove both his hands into the pizza box, making the jittery, excited sounds of a feral animal, clutching the crusts of two narrow, gooey slices, and dragging a golden-brown trail of molten cheese from the box to his plate, before barking up at her in response, "*I'M STARVED!*" and chomping into his pizza with cartoonish frenzy, his cheeks puffed to capacity with unswallowed bites.

His mother laughed. "*Wow,* okay! Just slow down there, wild-child! Don't want you to choke." She cracked his soda can open and slid it across the table to him. "Now… What was so weird about your day, kiddo?"

He chewed down the bites stuffed in his cheeks and washed them down with several loud gulps from his can, then he leaned forward in his seat and released an extended burp that was so intense, it seemed to paralyze his whole face in its open-mouthed position throughout its duration, to which his mother just rolled her eyes and sighed.

Brennan giggled and excused himself, covering his mouth with his hand, then said, "Okay, so, like, basically… We got this new kid in our class today. And he's pretty much regular looking, only he's little still little—*little'er* than everyone else, I mean— cause he's not really supposed to be a real fifth grader like me, he's actually supposed to be a *fourth*-grader, but he's *so* super smart, they had to move him up to my grade..."

—　　　　—　　　　—　　　　—　　　　—

In the time leading up to the father coming home, Brennan's mother—who, by that point, was already three slices into her dinner and sitting down to a fresh third cocktail—had been quite lively and animated in her conversation with her son, unpacking the major events of his day and giving him her preliminary thoughts on the subject—gesturing all the while with broad swings of her arms, and even letting some colorful language slip that she wouldn't normally use in front of the boy.

Then, once she heard her husband's keys jingling on the doorstep outside, she froze silent, mid-word, dropping whatever line of thought she seemed so passionate about only moments before, as though she'd fallen into some kind of prey-animal trance. She went rigid then, sitting bolt upright in her chair, rolling her shoulders back, and fidgeting with the loose strands of hair that looped down around her face and plucking them from the sticky corners of her mouth before tucking them back behind her ears and clasping her hands on the table in front of her, just as the front door opened.

To Brennan, it seemed as though she was *pretending* like she had been sitting in total silence with him before his father came home. He figured it was some kind of joke—even if he didn't understand what the joke was—but he went along with her charade anyway, mirroring her stiff posture and clasped hands.

The father entered, staring slack-jawed and furrow-browed at the scene in the kitchen, and slowly closed the door behind him, pivoting and sliding his first arm free of its coat sleeve. "Oh, *boy*... W-what's all *this* about—or should I be afraid to even ask...?" But before either of them could respond, his eyes got big and he began shaking his head, tossing his coat over the arm of the couch and throwing up his hands, swirling them through the air like an orchestra conductor, before they finally came down to perch on his hips, and through a humorless, scrunched-up smile that raised his cheeks up to his nostrils, he said, "Oh, *wait!* Oh, God—just wait! Don't even tell me, let me guess... The boy's in trouble—*once a-gain!*—only *this* time, little miss molly-coddling *mommy* here thought she'd treat him to a nice little pizza party because—*what?*—you *feel bad...* Is that it? Did I get it?" He wilted the words "feel bad" so they carried a mocking sting, hunching down to his son's eye-level with a clownlike frown, twisting his fists in his eye sockets as a pantomime of crying before he straightened himself and continued. "Well, go on then... You might as well give it to me straight, doc... What was it this time, *huh?* Is it grades, or what? Or are you bullying someone now—is *that* what it is? *Huh?* Can't imagine a little putz like you already having any *girl* trouble—*heaven forbid*—and we'd know in a heartbeat if you were ever on drugs, so—*wait...* Oh, you had *better* not be telling me that you've been mouthing off to your teacher again—because we *talked* about that already. A *few* times now, I think—wouldn't you say?"

"Well, yessir, father-sir, we did. And I know better than to talk back to Mr. Q, sir. But if you can just gimme a second so I can—"

"—So you can, *what*, huh? *Explain?*" he said, throwing his hands up in exasperation, "Well, that's only what I've been· *trying* to get out of you ever since I walked through that door!"

The boy had never heard the expression *deja-vu* before, and he knew of no other words or ways to express the unshakable feeling that he was reliving an event that he had already lived-through—having gone through an eerily similar exchange just an hour earlier with his mother. No, in the boy's limited vocabulary, he simply interpreted the combination of feelings, thoughts, and emotions he was experiencing as: '*I know I'm not dreaming right now, and this feels way too weird to be real life, so I must just be going some kind of crazy.*'

Brennan wanted to talk, to respond in a way that would make his father stop and listen. He knew that if he could just say the right thing and make the man understand the truth—that everything was alright and he didn't get into any trouble at all—

then he could help the man calm right back down and they could have the nice night together that he had planned. But despite his efforts, Brennan couldn't bring himself to do more than sputter a few half-worded phrases, disjointed and all out of context, in his desperate attempt to reassure a parent—for the second time that day—that he had not, in fact, done anything to get in trouble. Only *this* time, with his father, the heartbeat-pulse pounding away in his temples felt like a vice-grip around his head, squeezing all the thoughts out of his brain. With each stuttering attempt at defense or reassurance, his father's irritation only grew worse, with each reply coming louder and more intense than the one before.

Brennan kept darting his eyes over to his mother, trying to signal her to step in and say something, to tell him that she had already had a shorter, quieter version of this same, sad conversation earlier, and that—*really*—he only wanted to talk with them about something on his mind.

But she remained silent, sitting motionless in that same position she had been holding since her husband arrived—except for the occasional roll of her eyes whenever he said something that she found either absurd, laughable, or *rich-coming-from*-him. She held a sly smirk on her face as she slowly closed her eyes and opened them, blinking like a late-night driver dozing off behind the wheel.

The irony of hearing a harsher, louder version of her own earlier miscommunication with her son—repeated live, practically beat-for-beat, right in front of her—was entirely lost on the mother, who could only scoff and shake her head in disbelief at what a puffed-up, overbearing, and self-important little man she'd married.

When the father finally noticed the boy's nervous, sideways glances to his mother, he turned to her, then back at the boy. "Uhh, why are you...? What is this? Why's he keep looking at you? Is there something you'd like to add to help clarify things here? 'Cause I can't make heads or tails out of anything this kid's telling me."

It was then that the mother finally moved, unclasping her hands with geisha stillness to reach for her third cocktail without so much as a glance in her husband's direction, ice tinkling in her unsteady grip as she raised it and took a sip. "Well, y'know... Maybe if you'd *shut-the-hell-up* a minute and let someone *else* talk for a change... We could've told you that there really *was* nothing to worry about—nothing at all. In *fact*, I think you'll get quite a kick out of what our son wants to tell us... Come on, sit down... Your loving wife was even nice enough to pour you a drink—it's waiting for you in the fridge. Trust me, you're gonna *want* it for this one..."

The father grunted, shrugged, then slumped into the kitchen.

Brennan heard the fridge door open, then close, and moments later, the man rounded the corner with his drink and pulled up the empty seat between the boy and his mother. "Well, son, if what your mother says is true, then I'm afraid I owe you an apology for doubting you," he reached across them both to serve himself some still-warm pizza. "Even adults make mistakes sometimes, boy, and I'm not too big to admit when I'm wrong about something."

"It's okay. It's fine," Brennan said, shrugging.

"So, tell me, what's this big, earth-shaking announcement you have for us, huh? Something good, I hope?"

"Well, I already told mom some of it," Brennan said, looking down at the sticks of pizza crust on his plate, "but basically, we got this new kid in our class today, and he's really nice, and he's *super* smart, and at breaktime today, he—"

"—And he's a no-good little *liar*, that's what!" The mother cut in, slapping her hand down to the table with a *THUMP* as she said the word, 'liar'.

The father's brows leapt and he took a drink from his glass. "Whoa, all that, huh? So, what was this big lie he was going around telling everyone?"

"Well, I don't really know for *sure* that the kid was lying— that's just what mom and maybe a couple other kids think. But he was really smart and nice, and just a regular good-boy kid like me. Like, someone I'd probably wanna be friends with. Even though he's still littler than me, I think he's prolly smarter than me—or at least, like, the same amount of smart as me—so that makes us even. And he seemed really honest, too, so I don't really think he—"

"—Oh, *please!*" the mother cut in once more, slurping from her glass before continuing, "Don't be a *rube*, kiddo. Anyone can *seem* honest! That's why the whole world's run by crooks!"

"Jesus, *hon*—can... Can you just *stop* with this, already?" the father said. "I'm trying to get the straight story outta this kid, but I can't make out one iota of what happened with you *squawking on* endlessly like this."

The mother shrugged and put up her hands in surrender. Grinning, she motioned with pinched fingers like she was zipping her lips together, then she crossed her arms and slumped back in her chair. When nobody spoke up for a moment, she eyeballed her son and swept an arm in her husband's direction, urging him to proceed.

"Well, okay... So, like, at breaktime today," the boy said after a moment, trying to collect his thoughts through the swirling noise in his head, "me and a bunch of other kids all met up to talk to this new kid and ask him stuff, and he was telling us about, like, how he skipped a grade to be in our class, even though he's not as old as us, and we—"

"—And some of the other kids thought he might've been lying..." The father chuckled, shaking his head with relief. "Son, sometimes kids really *do* skip grades. It's really not all that uncommon. Every once in a while, some brainy little wünderkind comes along who's that little bit smarter than his peers, works a little bit harder, and—"

"—*No*, daddy—er, *father-sir*—*that's* not the part they thought he was lying about. Mr. Q already *told us* that he skipped a grade. It's what he said *after* that."

"Oh, I see," the father said, nodding his head and taking a long drink.

"Yeah, so, like, we were all just talking, asking him what kinda stuff he likes, but then *one* kid asked him what his parents hit him with, and *he* said that they don't hit him with anything. Not their hand, not *nothin'*. Like, *ever*. Not even when he's bad."

The father sputtered a restrained cough as he choked and gasped momentarily on his bite of pizza. He pounded on his chest until he'd dislodged the doughy lump, clearing his throat with a series of forceful grumbles—*like a revving lawn mower*, Brennan thought—before washing it all down with his drink. "*Mm...* Okay, so this kid's trying to go around saying that his folks never hit him, huh? And then you and your friends all saw right through it? Okay, good. Got it. *Continue.*"

"Oh, uh... Okay... So then, at lunchtime, we went back to the tree and talked to him again and said, like, *'well, what do you mean?'* and he was like, *'they just don't hit me,'* so then we were like, *'Well, what do they do to you when you're bad?'* and then he said all this stuff about how his parents don't ever think he's a *'bad'* boy, and that they trust him and know that he's really a good boy—like, on the *inside*—and so, whenever they have problems, they all just talk with each other and work it all out, and... Well, anyway, I guess that's pretty much it."

"*Whoo...*" the father said, staring up at the ceiling and shaking his head, "Well, I can see now why you thought I'd need a drink for this one. I think I'll go and freshen this one up while I figure out how to respond to such nonsense."

He drained the rest of his drink in a single gulp, then got up to take his glass to the kitchen.

"*Ugh—thank* you!" the mother piped up, smacking the table once more for emphasis, "It *is* nonsense—*complete* nonsense! And that's what I told him, as well! —Actually, *wait*, hold up a sec, hon—I'll come and top mine off, too." She scooped up her glass and downed the remaining third in several chugging gulps, then burped as she pushed her chair back and jogged to the kitchen to meet her husband.

Brennan heard his mother's voice continuing in the kitchen, saying, "But yeah, that's exactly what I told him when I heard that—simply *ridiculous!* Like, what kind of *fairy tale world* is that kid living in?"

Then her voice took on a saccharine cooing quality, making her sound more 'child-*ish*' than actually 'like a child', saying, "'*Oh, no-o-o-o, my perfect parents would never do something as evil as* 'spanking' *their sweet, precious angel. No-o-o, my parents have nice, cushy jobs, so they can send me away to private schools and hire maids and nannies and butlers to raise and discipline me-e-e... And since they never have to actually* deal *with me, they're always so nice and happy and never stressed out—isn't that just so great for me-e-e-e?*'—Ugh, *please!* Don't make me puke. Y'know, I don't know a single other parent—not a *single* one—who doesn't have to... You know... '*Lay-down-the-law*' on their kids every once in a while... And, for that matter, I haven't met a kid yet who couldn't use a good swatting every once in a while—I mean, only when they *deserve* it, of course—but still, it's... It's necessary. Maintains discipline. Respect. All that good stuff." The mother nodded to herself, then gulped down another swig. "Somebody ought to tell *Mr. & Mrs. Perfect* over there that *some* of us actually have to *work* for a living, and *excu-u-use me* if we're just out here just trying to do the best we can with what little we have."

"Mm hmm..." was the father's only reply as he returned to the dining room table with his drink and sat down. He had filled his drink high and slurped some of it off the top before setting it down on the table to avoid spilling, then he turned his chair to face Brennan, legs crossed and arm slung over the chair's back. "So, tell me, son: what're *your* thoughts on all this?"

"*Oh*, uhh... Well, I don't... I guess, I don't really know..." It was a simple-enough question, asked in a calm, gentle-enough tone—and, if it were anybody else doing the asking, Brennan would have been pleased to hear an adult asking him about his thoughts—but knowing that the question came from his father made his back feel almost *minty*-cold, like stepping out of a shower and getting blasted by an air-conditioner. He shrugged his shoulders continually, opening and closing his mouth as though he was trying to speak, then instantly changing his mind each time, looking like an animatronic with faulty wiring. When he finally spoke, he said, "I just… Nothing, I guess."

"'*Nothin'*,' huh?" The father huffed a laugh, then smiled, licking the teeth at the high corner of his mouth. He grabbed the edge of his seat and scooted his chair closer to his son, then leaned in, patting the boy's knee a couple times, rubbing his kneecap with his thumb and then giving it a little shake before leaning back in his chair. "Can I just ask: what exactly do you *mean* when you say, '*nothin*'? Huh? Is that all you got in there between your ears? A great big *nothin*? Huh? Well, I can't speak for your mother here, but I know *I* sure didn't raise some brainless, know-nothin' dummy… So I just need to know if either, *A*, you're lying to me right *now*—and you *do*, in fact, have some thoughts in that head of yours about this business with the new kid—or *B*, you've been lying to me, and you're not *really* my son, but just some random zombie kid in off the street who only happens to *look* like my son—some *stranger* that we've just been feeding and taking care of for free all these years. So, which is it then, huh? You tell me."

"Oh, calm down, *you*—ya big grump!" the mother called from the kitchen, a playful scold in her voice, as though he'd just barked at their son for walking in front of the TV during a big game. She rounded the corner into the dining room, holding her glass up to her eye level with both hands, glancing away from it only briefly enough to shoot scornful glances at her husband "You ease off of the boy; he's probably just sick of talking about it, is all. I mean, God, just *look* at him! *See?* You're making him nervous! Don't you let him bother you, sweetie—he's just letting off steam. That's all."

Brennan's arms trembled so hard that he had to grab his elbows and dig his forearms down into his belly to keep them still. His eyes still trained on his pizza crusts, he shrugged once more, saying, "I'm fine," before realizing that neither of his parents would accept that answer without pressing further, so he forced himself to say *something* else, even if he couldn't bring himself to look up from his empty plate to say it. "I-I… Well, I mean—okay, like, I guess I have *some* thoughts about the new kid… But nothing *bad* though. Mostly just that I think he's cool and smart and lucky that he got to skip a grade and lucky that his, uhh—well, you know… Lucky that he doesn't get hit ever. But that's all though. That's all the thoughts I have. Is that okay? Was that enough thoughts?"

"You did fine, sweetie," the mother said, "Don't let this old *grump* scare you." Then she reached across the table to where her husband was drumming his fingers and swatted the back of his knuckles, as though scolding him for trying to snatch food off her plate.

"Yeah, that was fine, son," the father said, "I just hope that wasn't too hard for you—opening up your mouth and actually telling me what you *think* about something for once, and not your usual zombie responses, like, '*Eh. Oh. Uh. Yea. It was okay. It was fine.*' You didn't *strain* anything there, did you, boy?"

The father chuckled into his drink at his own remark, but Brennan shook his head as a reflex, not fully understanding the question.

The mother turned to face her husband, pointing a finger at him.

"Well, I don't know about *you, Mister Grump*, but when he told me about all this earlier, and he asked me—said he wanted to know what *I* thought about this *so-called* new kid—well, I went ahead and I told him the *truth*," the mother said, nodding and raising her glass above her head in a toast to no one in particular, sloshing an orange wave against the wall of the glass, sending it crashing up and over its lip, sprinkling down onto to the table and misting the boy's forehead and cheeks. "I told him, straight-up, I said: 'this new kid might have skipped a grade—hell, he might've skipped a *hundred* grades, for all I care—but all that really says is that he knows how to work the system, because, at the end of the day, he's still *obviously* nothing more than a bald-faced little liar. And I'm *so-rry* to be so blunt—I know it's not exactly *pee-see* to speak your mind these days—but that really *is* the way I see it, and there's nothing out there's gonna change my mind. I'm just being honest and telling the truth here—and the truth isn't always sunshine-and-margaritas. More often than not, the truth is just a firm slap across the face to remind us of our raising. And the truth is that *no parent* can handle a child without the occasional need for discipline—and, *yes*, sometimes that discipline means a kid might need a little swat-on-the-butt or something to set him straight. But, I guess me saying that *already* means that I'm a terrible, no-good mother—just sitting around all day watching soaps, eating bonbons, milking unemployment, and letting my kid *starve-to-death*... Isn't that right, kiddo?"

Brennan's brows leapt at the prompt. "*Whuh*—no! No *way*, mommy! You'd *never* do any of that bad stuff!"

"Well, that may be, but that's exactly what the *pee-see police* would sure have you think of me! Honestly, it's just incredible to me that these schools are allowed to indoctrinate our own children against us, twisting their minds around every which-way until they hate their own parents. Just makes me sick! But I don't know—maybe that's just *me?*" She slurped her drink through the gaps in the ice until the cubes stuck to the bottom tumbled down to her mouth, splashing the orange liquid against her lips and dribbling it down her chin and onto her shirt.

"Oh, *no*, mommy! Please don't say that! I could *never* hate you! Even if they told me—even if *Mr. Q* told me that I had to hate you, or else he would beat up everyone in the classroom—I *still* wouldn't do it, not for one second!"

"Well, I know *that*, but that's only 'cause we raised you to be such a super-smart little sweetie. And *we* tell you the truth, even when the truth is *hard*—unlike *some* of these radical snowflake parents you hear about out there. You're lucky, if I'm being honest, most kids' parents don't even tell them the *real* truth about the world—they just play make-believe in some little rainbow-unicorn fantasy until the kids are all grown up and try to make it out there in the real world—then it's *wake-up time*. All I've got to say to those woke little future trust-fund brats is two words: '*Good. Luck.*' 'Cause they're *sure* gonna need it."

After a beat of silence, the mother caught her husband looking down, stone-faced and mesmerized. His elbow was propped on the table, wrist bent, suspending and gently swirling the drink suspended between his fingertips, gazing down into his glass like it could reveal his future. She nudged the back of his hand with the moist outer wall of her glass. "Hey, you still with us there, *Mr. Grump?*"

"Mm," the father said, looking up at her, then back down to his drink before taking another sip, "Yeah. Still here. I've just been collecting my thoughts. I don't feel the need to say every half-formed thought out loud the second it crosses my mind, like *some* people do."

"Oh, well, then, by all means—please, enlighten us, *Mr. Free-Thinking Philosopher!* What great thoughts are going on in that dusty ol' noodle of yours?"

"Well, I probably already know what you're gonna say, anyway," Brennan said before his father had a chance to respond, stacking small fists on the table and resting his chin down atop them. "I bet you probably think he's lying too, huh?"

"Well, son, my answer might end up surprising you," the father said, setting his drink down and adjusting his position into a kind of seated crouch, facing the boy while also glancing occasionally at his wife, "But, no. I *don't* necessarily think he's lying. I mean, who knows? Maybe his parents just beat the *fear-of-God* into him back when he was still too young to remember. And that's really the way to do it, if you ask me. Let 'em know you mean business right out the gate when they're young, and they'll know better than to shirk and backtalk. So, maybe they just never needed to do it again? But, then again, maybe he *does* actually have a pair of those deranged, new-age, hippy-dippy liberals for parents who think that *their* kids walk on water and their farts don't stink."

Brennan cracked up at that last line.

"And if *that* is the case, then, well..." the father paused, sighing, pursing his lips and shaking his downcast head, as though he had sorrowful news to report. "...Let's just say, they might not be *'hitting him,'* exactly, but what they're doing to that boy is far worse in the long-run than any licking from any belt—I can tell you that much right now. *Talking* is all well and good, but a lot of kids—as *you* well know, son—just won't *listen*, no matter *how much* talking you do. And talking alone won't teach you any of the *hard* lessons in life. Like how to stand up after you fall down, or that actions have consequences, or that life isn't *fair* or *nice*, and that the world's a bad place full of bad, nasty, evil, selfish people who simply couldn't care less about you—and if you want any chance of surviving it, you'll have to get a little of that same meanness in you, too, and fight for anything you want in this world, and then you'll have to fight to *keep* everything that's rightfully yours. It might not be some pretty cartoon, with talking mice and birds and crap—but hey, *that's* the real world for ya, whether we like it or not! But you just mark my words and you *wait* until that kid's in high school—*ooh*, I can see it, clear as day—greasy long hair, hunched-over posture—I'm talking *zero* upper-body strength—shirking his studies, just hangin' out with his greasy little burn-out buddies behind the handball courts, cutting classes, doing dope, and—you know— going to all those anti-establishment protests, and all that mob-mentality malarkey. Just *no* respect for authority whatsoever—or anything *else* that makes this country great. People like that—if I can even *call* 'em 'people'—are more interested in *looking* good and *pretending* to be decent, hard-working, God-fearing people than they are in actually putting in the time and the work of *being* decent people—and that all just makes me sick, just sick-to-my-stomach. All this so-called '*gentle parenting*,' *goo-goo-ga-ga*, commie baloney BS that they're stuffing down this idiot kid's throat—all this, '*Oh, but all that willy matters is pwotecting the poor kid's pwecious fee-wings; oh, we mustn't hurt their poor fee-wings!*—it all plays out *exactly* like Socialism: looks nice and great on paper, but it's an utter *disaster* in real life. Just you mark my words and watch—I mean, just look at what's going on with that whole mess in Venezuela, for crying out loud! Or *Cuba*, for that matter—*hel-lo!*"

He then slumped over, bracing his forearms on the table and shaking his drooped head. He kept his eyes popped wide open, staring straight down, point-blank, into nothing but the smudged white of his plate, shaking his head and rocking himself, gently, back and forth in his seat. Then he slapped his palms against the table and propped himself up with a loud inhale, grabbed his drink and knocked it back, downing it while holding a couple of fingers up between his lips and nose to block the ice while he gulped. When it was empty, he tilted it away from him, licking his lips and adding a refreshed, '*aaah,*' then he turned to face the other two with a smile so big and tight-lipped, they instinctively knew it was not a '*happy*' smile, but neither of them could pin down exactly what the father was thinking or feeling.

Still gripping his glass, he pushed his chair back and rose, dashing off toward the kitchen and disappearing around the corner in long, heavy strides.

"Oh, wait, here, actually—wait, hon, before you go… *Hon?*" the mother said, pausing for a response, with her arm already fully extended in her husband's direction—even though he'd already disappeared around the corner—holding out her glass to him, wagging it from side to side as the craggy, melting mound of orange-stained ice remained stuck to the bottom of the glass. "…Uh—*hello?* Hon? …Do you think you could get your beautiful, loving wife a little topper?"

Her husband reappeared with a sidestep from the kitchen, squinting down at his wife with a stern mask of austere suspicion, saying, "Mm… Well, that depends… How much would you say you've already *had* this evening? Are you sure you really need any more?"

—   —   —   —   —

That intimidating mask was the same familiar face that Brennan received earlier in the evening when he first told his father that he wanted to talk—as well as virtually every other time they had to interact for longer than the span of a 15-minute car ride over that last year. Whether they were 'disciplinary interactions' or fun weekend adventures, or even just on weekly outings to their Sunday church services, that scary face of his was always locked, loaded, and eager to be released. No matter where they went or what the other two said or did, before long, something small would inevitably set him off out of nowhere, leaving him rubbing his face, pacing, stomping, raising his voice, flinging insults, and generally looking like he wanted to hit something or somebody.

As instantly recognizable as that face was to his wife and son, it was a mask that the father himself had also—without ever even realizing it—grown quite comfortable wearing.

Of course, he would never admit to such a strange, offensive notion, but if he looked deeply enough inside himself, he would soon reach the undeniable conclusion that this same angry mask that came so easily and naturally to him, with its own angry posture and tone-of-voice, had always lent him a certain sense of comfort and control, just as it had since he was a boy.

The rush of hot energy flooding his face and chest. The familiar tension burning throughout every muscle in his jaw, brows, and forehead. The fidgeting satisfaction of grinding his teeth whenever he had to listen to anyone else speak for longer than a simple greeting. And now, as an adult with his *own* family, he finally had the ability to actually *say* everything that was on his mind to people who didn't have the power to make his life any more difficult than it already was. That mask, and the voice it produced, always made him feel a little bit stronger, more in-control—powerful in a way that he wasn't really *allowed* to feel at work without risking consequences that could force himself and his family out onto the streets, homeless and starving in a matter of months, if not weeks.

From a young age, and all throughout his childhood, Brennan's father was raised to believe that *anger* was the only worthwhile emotion, and that all the other '*feelings*' were nothing more than a waste of time, because—as his own father so frequently put it—'Anger's *good!* People *listen* to anger! Anger actually *gets stuff done!* So, growing up, any time Brennan's father felt sad or frustrated, disappointed or confused—or any of the other feelings that his father regarded as one of the "weak" emotions—he would train his mind to simply search out and gather up all of the things about his situation that he could be angry about, then he would focus his attention on *those* things, like ants under the spotlight of a magnifying glass, until all those other uncomfortable feelings withered and faded away, leaving nothing behind but their angry ghosts, with their own angry shapes and thoughts and opinions.

Now, as an adult, Brennan's father—like most fathers—is determined to do a better job of raising his own son than his father did with him. But despite his attempts to set himself apart from his own father's teachings and methods, he always carried that trinity of his father's valued beliefs burning in his heart: *Anger's good. People listen to anger. Anger gets stuff done.*

—   —   —   —   —

"Well, it is precisely none of your *business* how much I've had to drink, *Mr. Grump*," the mother said, looking away from the man with a haughty pout. "I'm a big girl, if you haven't noticed, fully grown, and I have had a *long* day at work, so when I say, mommy's thirsty... *That* means, you go run along and get mommy her little drink. *Capiche?* Now, go on. You be a good boy now and scoot."

The father rolled his eyes at her, swiping the glass out of her hand and shaking his head as he walked away.

The mother chuckled into the back of her wrist, then turned to Brennan. "*Any-way*... I think what your father was *trying* to say, hon," she said, resting her fingers on the boy's shoulder, "is that we only ever do what we do *because* we love you. Because we *care*. You know that, don't you, sweetie? Right? We just want to make sure that you grow up good and strong, get a good job, marry a good woman, and be a good husband and provider someday—a real *leader*, you know? Someone others can look up to. Not just some spoiled little silver-spoon know-nothing who thinks the world-owes-'em-a-living. So, when we have to tell you 'no' sometimes, or scold you, or say something that makes you sad, or mad at us—*believe* me—it's only *ever* for your own good. Like... You remember last year, around Christmas time, when you were down sick with that bad flu, and you threw up into the church offering basket? And then we rushed you home and made you drink that nasty, disgusting medicine—oh, you *hated* that stuff! You remember that? Boy, you were kicking and screaming, throwing such a little hissy-fit, saying, '*No, no, no! Just let me stay sick! I wanna stay sick!*' But you *did* eventually take the medicine, and—even though it didn't taste or feel too good at the time—once it had a chance to do its work inside you... Then you got better real fast, and—look at you *now*—you turned out A-O-K! You remember that? Well, that's how it is sometimes trying to be a parent... Or even kinda like that one superhero you love so much—'*Violence Man,*' or whatever his stupid name is."

"*Vengeance* Man," Brennan said, snickering at her mistake.

"Right, *him.* Well, you know how, sometimes, even Vengeance Man has to do things that hurt people or make people sad—people like the *bad guys*—to make sure that everyone else— all the *good* and *normal* people—are safe and protected? That's how it is whenever your father or I have to do something that hurts *your* feelings when you're bad. We never *want* to scold you, or say '*no*' to you, or tell you that you're not allowed to do something—and we would never-in-a-million-years even *dream* of hitting you for anything unless you *absolutely* deserved it... *But,* we also don't want you growing into some spoiled little brat, either—some pampered little snowflake who's had everything handed to him on a silver-spoon and never had to work a day in his life for anything, and has zero idea what the *real world* is like out there. So, if making sure you grow up right means that every once in a while, when you're extra, extra bad, either your father or I have to bend you over and give you a little swat on the bottom... Well, then I guess I must just be the worst mother in the whole world. *Oh well...* I tried my best." She grimaced and shrugged, tossing her hands in the air and looking about as upset as if she had just missed a backyard frisbee catch.

Brennan shook his head frantically, then hopped out of his seat and lunged at his mother, wrapping his arms around her and holding her tight. "Oh, *no*, mommy! Never, *never* say that! You're the *best* mommy in the whole world!" His eyes were on the verge of tears when his father's heavy steps rounded the corner with the two tinkling glasses—one blink, and they'd be streaming down his cheeks—but he knew the man would not appreciate the sight, so he detached himself from his mother's side and backed into his seat, drying his face with the backs and heels of his hands, then he sniffed back hard and gulped down the gooey warmth collecting at the back of his throat. When he looked up, his father was frozen in place a few steps from the table, with a look on his face like he had just walked in on them dissecting a live frog, before rolling his eyes at the scene and setting a drink down in front of his wife.

When she leaned in to reach for it, he slid the glass back toward himself, saying, "Look, now I don't care *how much* you drink—you can go ahead and drink yourself into oblivion, if that's what you want—but I am *not* waking up at two-ay-em again and stepping in, or cleaning up, any of your little '*drinking messes*' ever again—*comprendé?* If you don't know when to stop, then that's on you. Now… That is all I have to say on the subject, and I consider the matter closed."

A beat of silence passed between them all, then, once he felt his point had received adequate time to sink in, he finally nodded at his wife and slid the glass back in front of her.

She smirked and raised an eyebrow at him, equally unimpressed by the man's proclamation and his theatrics with her drink. Her features all sunk into a dour parody of seriousness as she shot a rigid hand up at an angle against her forehead, then she shot off her salute, adding in a deep, clowny voice, sounding like a barking seal, "*Oh, yes sir, Mr. Grump, sir! Whatever you say, sir!*"—which cracked up their son, even though he ducked his smile behind his hand. She then raised her glass and took a long sip before remembering something that nearly made her spit her drink back into her glass, and said, "*Oh*, and by the way, I noticed that you put your crusty ol' fingernails in my drink just now, so—you know—*thanks for that.*" She scrunched up her face, sticking out her tongue and scraping it against her top teeth, then she swigged down another gulp while glaring at the man.

The husband didn't respond, or even look up to notice the look she was giving him. He was staring back down into his glass again, stirring the ice and amber concoction with his fingertip.

Brennan lifted the pizza cover, reaching for another slice, saying, "So, like, uh… Oh, *wait—shoot!*—sorry!" He froze, his eyes wide and darting between the two parents, the slice still drooping from his fingers. "Am I allowed to, uh—like, is it okay for me—I mean, can I talk now? Are you guys done?"

The mother snorted a small laugh that sounded like a flat, "*Heh*," still scowling at her husband over the rim of her glass, and said to Brennan without budging her gaze, "Of *course*, sweetie. Trust me, I don't think your father's going to say anything worthwhile again for the foreseeable future. So what is it? What's on your mind, sweetie?" She took another sip, set her glass down, and slowly turned her head to face her son.

Brennan nodded his head a few times, sighing so big, it felt like he forgot to breathe for a few seconds. He raised the limp slice with both hands, careful not to disturb the lump of melted mozzarella that had cooled into a coagulated dollop dangling from its tip, and laid it onto his plate. Then he plucked off the cheese lump and stuffed it in his mouth. "Okay, so, like… Either way…" he said, chewing and licking his fingers before continuing, "…You guys don't think he's a very good boy, right? Like, on the *inside?* I get that *you* think that he really *does* get hit," he said, pointing to his mother, "and that he's just lying about it to everybody so he can *look* good…" then he turned his finger to his father, saying, "And you think that he *might* be lying, but even if he's not lying, then he's still messed up in, like, a *crazy*-kind-of-way, and he's going to end up like a *really* bad person when he grows up… *Right?* …Did I get all that right?"

"—*Yes,* uh-huh. Exactly," said the mother.

"—Well, not *entirely*, no—but I suppose you got the general idea," said the father.

"Well, that—I mean, *that*… That's just so… Messed *up!* …I mean, like, *why?* He seemed like such a nice kid… I just don't get *why* someone who seemed so nice would want to do something

like that, and lie to us all about something so—so... *Not nice...*"
Brennan glanced at each parent, hoping one of them might step in,
cutting him off in order to provide some comforting resolution to
his turmoil, but when none came, he drooped his head and sunk
his shoulders forward, letting out a long, quiet sigh, and deflating
in on himself.

If what his parents were telling him was true, he couldn't
think of anything else he could possibly say to express the spirit-
dampening disappointment he felt toward that new kid.

"...Look," the father said, "maybe he *is* lying, maybe he's
not—but the fact remains that some kids just can't face facts with
reality and turn into delusional liars. And from what you're
telling us, this kid sounds like he's being raised by a real couple of
fruit loops. But whether he's *lying* or not, and whether they *hit*
him or not, are all beside the point. The only thing you really
need to remember about anything you heard here tonight is that
some kids out there got it *way* worse off than you. And also, that
you should just be *grateful* to have such honest parents who tell
you the truth about the way the *real world* works and don't
sugarcoat it." He looked back down at his drink, uncertain if
there was some other, *third* message he wanted Brennan to walk
away with, but when he couldn't come up with anything, he took
another drink and continued with the first thing that came to his
mind, saying, "...But, *o-o-ohh*, you just watch, I'm telling you, in
just a few short years, that kid's either gonna wind up dead, or
gay, or in prison before he's even fully grown—you mark my
words."

"I hate to say it, sweetie, but... I think your father might be
right on this one. It's probably best you stay away from that kid
from now on. And I'm not saying it's necessarily his *fault*, you
know what I mean? Like, I'm sure he might *seem* like a nice,
good, regular little boy, but some of these parents can really mess
up their kids *bad*—without even realizing it or meaning to. And
we think it's just for the best—your father and I—that you avoid
those types of *strange* and *off-putting* kinds of people... I mean,
when you're a little bit older and you see a little more of life, you
learn time-after-time that nobody's ever *really* good. Not *deep*

down, anyway. And, whether we like it or not, all you little kiddos just *suck up* our bad habits like hungry little vacuums—so we're all pretty much doomed, right out the gate." She laughed at her own grim humor, then took another swig and leaned in so close to Brennan, her breath stung the inside of his nose. "It's like my mother always said to me, kiddo: 'There's only one man who was ever truly good—and they nailed *Him* to a cross!' As for the rest of us... We're all just... Floating around through life... Doing the best we can while *pretending* to be these good, nice people who never get mad or upset or sick-to-death of the way things are run. So, yeah... It might not be pretty, but that's the *truth*. Easier for most people to just go along playing *make-believe* that we live in a nice, caring world than admitting that, deep down, beneath all the phony-baloney smiles and the nice how-do-ya-do's, we're all just made of the same ol' mean and selfish stuff, ready to stomp on anyone who gets in our way. Everything else is just an act."

"Uh-huh..." Brennan said, nodding along and squinting off to one side as he tried to put it all together. "Okay... But, like... I mean... *I'm* still a good boy, right?"

The father chuckled into his lap, then scooted his chair in closer and leaned in, bracing a hand against each of his knees so that his rigid arms propped his shoulders up to his ears, making him look, from the knees up, like a perching gargoyle.

"Well, son," the father said, "this is maybe an excellent opportunity for you to stop and think to yourself for a second about that very question: would a so-called '*good boy*' get in trouble as much as you do?"

The question melted Brennan's guts, and they all seeped down, into a heavy pool collecting at the very bottom of his belly. "Bu-but, *no*... But... I never *try* to get in any trouble—*never!*"

"Aw, well, we know that, sweetie," the mother said, offering Brennan a sympathetic frown and placing her hand between her son's shoulder blades, rubbing his neck between her thumb and fingers. "But none of us ever *try* to get in trouble—do we, pumpkin? Some people just can't help themselves. But, I think that's pretty normal at your age. So... While you might not be a 'good boy', exactly, you're hardly a 'bad' boy—especially considering some of the *vile* things other boys can get up to... But I want you to know, no matter how much trouble you ever get yourself into, you'll still always be my little boy—no matter what. You could go on a nationwide killing spree and become *America's Most Wanted*, and you'd *still* be your momma's little boy... I only ask that you please never do anything to... *Embarrass* us... That's all I ask... And besides, you're still young now, so, hopefully, you'll just... You know... Grow out of it."

"Oh," said Brennan, blinking, unable to take his eyes off of the untouched slice on his plate. "Um, okay. Yeah, I... I guess I'll probably just grow out of it..." Then he raised his head and looked back up at them, suddenly bright and beaming. "Yeah, that makes sense! I'll just grow-out-of-it! I can do that! I *will*, I promise! Once I get just a little bit older, then I'll just grow-out-of-it, and I'll only ever be good again after that!"

His parents both shared a little laugh over their son's naïvety, exchanging warm glances with each other mid-laughter, and melting away the earlier tensions between them. If Brennan wasn't sitting between them, they might have even held hands.

"Oh, son," the father said, still smiling and shaking his head, "if only life could be that easy. Truth is, as we get older, life just keeps getting harder and more complicated, and it only gets more and more difficult to play nice with all the morons and numbskulls you have to deal with on a daily basis, and all that stuff just tends to make us all worse and worse and worse."

" *Yep.* Sad, but true, kiddo," the mother said, nodding, her face solemn, "we were probably all of us better when we were still kids. You can't mess your life up as bad when you're still a kid. But life just kinda has a way of..." She stared off into the middle distance, vaguely gesturing with a swirling hand through the air, as though the end of her thought was a scent she was wafting toward her, before looking back down at her son and completing her thought with a grim smile. "...It just has a way of *sucking the life out of you*, I guess..."

Brennan's face sagged even lower, thinking about how miserable his poor mommy must feel, and wishing there was something he could do to help put more life back into her, when she suddenly lit up, straightening in her seat, her eyes wide, and tapping her fingers against the tabletop in excitement.

"*Oh-oh-oh-oh-oh—!*" she said, adjusting herself in her seat and fidgeting with her appearance like she was preparing to give some announcement, "—and *speaking* of sucking-the-life-out-of-you... I have *got* to tell you guys about my day today—you won't believe it! Okay, so, I get to work, right, and the *first thing* I see when I get there—*right* as I'm walking through that door... Guess who's standing *right there* at reception, waiting for me to—oh, wait... I'm so sorry, honey, was there any more you wanted to tell us about that idiot new kid in your class, or..."

"Oh, uhh... Yeah, no, I guess not. Not really. That was pretty much it." Brennan shrugged, relieved at the change of subject, and finally raised the cold slice from his plate, chomping off a big bite, then after a few chews, he opened wide and asked through a garbled mouthful of dough and cheese, "*Sho, whah hoppont wiff yo dahh, mommeh?*"

"Aw, come on, son!" His father grimaced, blocking the sight with his hand before ultimately turning away. "We didn't raise you in no barn—cover your mouth when you talk, boy!"

Brennan covered his bulging mouth with his hand and giggled to himself, his voice coming out deeper than usual, sounding like, "*Huf, huf, huf,*" then he swallowed a portion of the bite and said through his cupped hand, "*Shaw-wee.*"

The father shook his head at the undignified display, but didn't let on any signs of his trademark anger. "This kid, I tell ya... So, as you were saying? You just got to work, and..."

"Right, okay, so... You know that stupid new regional-branch-whatever guy they brought in from who-knows-where to head up our department last quarter? *Well...*"

Brennan had trouble following his mother's story, and figured she was mostly telling it for his father's benefit, so as she spoke, his attention drifted back to thoughts of the new kid, as well as all of the big lessons he had learned from his parents that night. He still looked at whoever was talking between his bites of pizza, and he laughed whenever they laughed, and responded with exasperation whenever they did.

Once the mother finished her story, leaving all three of them groaning about the unfairness of her workday, she laughed and said, "*Eh*, but what can you do? The rich get richer, and the poor get children—am I right?"

She pulled another slice from the box and the father followed her lead, but she paused before taking her first bite, lowering it back down just above her plate. "Y'know, this is nice," she said. "All of us together like this, sitting around the table, eating and talking together like a *real* family. It's nice."

Brennan smiled and nodded his head, then attacked his next bite, snarling and tearing away at it like a ferocious animal, cracking up both of his parents.

—   —   —   —   —

His mother was right. There *was* something nice about all of them together like that—eating, laughing, enjoying each other's company, talking about their days, nobody fighting or yelling— and there was something special about the way that it *felt*, too. For the first time in more months than Brennan could remember, things felt like they did when he was still back in the fourth grade—maybe even the third grade. Before Mr. Q. Before he started getting into trouble all the time. Before his father's belt and his mother's pinches became almost weekly occurrences. Back when he could still believe he was a good boy. When he still *was* a good boy.

The mother raised her own slice up to her mouth and bit down a bigger bite than she usually would, trying to snarl and tear at it like her son had just done, but she lacked the unhinged gusto needed to convincingly pull off the gag. She looked up at the others, chipmunk-cheeked, to find both of them shaking their heads, their lips parted and mouths stretched tight into wide frowns—their expressions a combination of grimaces and goofy grins. She paused her ravenous eating sounds, a blank, nonchalant expression on her face, then she opened her mouth wide, revealing the pale pink wad of marinara-stained dough where her tongue should be, shrugging, asking, " *Whahf? Whah-ta-maht-ah?*"

At that, her husband and son erupted in groans of protest.

"Aw, *cringe*, mommy—*gross!*" Brennan laughed hard, cupping both hands over his mouth.

"Oh, *wow*. That's just... Real charming, hon. Guess I see now where he gets it from."

The mother kept gnawing, working the bite down until it became more manageable, then covered her mouth and said between bites, "Oh, what... Am I too *wild* for this family?"

Her husband laughed. "Oh, I'm afraid not, dear. It seems you've lived a life of domestication for far too long, grown too accustomed to our modern ways and comforts. You're too civilized now. They'd never accept you back in the wild now."

"Well, I guess the two of you are just stuck with me then." She reached over for her husband's hand, and he leaned in, extending his reach over the pizza box to meet hers. Their eyes met and the smiles that followed around the table warmed the entire room. She squeezed his hand tight, then released, caressing her thumb along the ridges of his knuckles. Using her free hand, she took another, regular-sized, bite of her pizza and turned to take in the sight of her son's beautiful smile as she chewed.

Come Brennan's bedtime, the household was as quiet as Mr. Q's classroom. But it was a *good* quiet. A calm, peaceful quiet, with none of the usual raised voices, stabbing each other with their unkind words. None of the slamming doors, rattling his body to the core like a shot through the gut.

As he nestled into his bed, making himself comfortable and adjusting his blankets the way he liked them, Brennan wondered whether or not his parents were still awake. They looked pretty sleepy, so perhaps they had simply walked through their door and passed out on the other side. Or, if they *were* somehow still awake, they must either be dead quiet or talking to each other so quietly, he couldn't make out as much as a murmur from their room.

If it had been any other night, the easy silence of the house would have helped him sleep as easily and soundly as he had after that day at the water park the previous summer, but after their dinner conversation, he couldn't stop thinking about that new kid at school. Brennan's mind bubbled over like a kitchen pot whenever his mother made pasta, thinking about what a mean person someone would have to be to make so many kids feel bad for something as normal and natural as spankings—even if they *were* older than him.

It's just not right, Brennan thought, *he shouldn't be allowed to get away with something as mean as all that. It just makes me sick-to-my-stomach. Maybe everybody really is bad—deep down on the inside—but this kid's extra-extra bad if he's doing all this mean stuff just to make himself feel extra good or smart or whatever. He may be smart at school stuff, but he's gotta be* extra *dumb about* real world *stuff if he still thinks he's a good boy. Tomorrow, I'm gonna go talk to that new kid and I'm gonna tell him that what he's doing is bad and mean to the rest of us kids, and that he's a bad person for lying so much, and that he has to stop or else there'll be trouble. Just like Vengeance Man.*

Eight.

A howling wind rattled Brennan's window all that next morning. Rain pounded the street outside, making each passing car sound like a tidal wave. The weather's noise was enough to wake him up long before he would usually rise for school, but he remained lying there in bed, replaying his thoughts from the previous night, over and over, until his alarm eventually went off. He peeked out through the blinds and knew it would be cold outside, so he bundled himself up, muscle-suit thick, in several layers of sweaters—but at no point while he was getting ready had he considered just how *wet* that morning's walk to school was going to be.

By the point in his walk where he could see the school's flagpole off in the distance, he was already pale and shivering, with all four layers of fabric soaked completely through to his skin, sopping like a soaked sponge.

The moment Mr. Q caught sight of Brennan's pitiful, bedraggled appearance sloshing his way a few steps into the classroom, the man rose from his desk and limped over to meet him, holding up his hand, stopping the boy in his tracks. "*Oh*, no! *Nope*, nuh-uh. You get out of here, *this instant*—you *go! Go, go, go!*"

Brennan's hands gripped their opposing biceps, squeezing them together hard to help steady their trembling, and slowly raised his head to face his teacher, trying to speak through chattering teeth, saying, "*Wh-wh... Wh*-where *d*-do you *w*-want me *t*-to *g-g-g*-go?"

"*Anywhere* else! The restroom, the nurse's office—hell, back outside in the rain, for all I care—just not *here*, not in my classroom! Now, just *go—please!*"

Brennan's legs were so cold and numb, he couldn't take any big steps, but he shuffled himself out into the hallway as quickly as his stiff little limbs could carry him, then, once out in the hall, he took his time making it the rest of the way to the nurse's office.

—　　　—　　　—　　　—　　　—

By the time Brennan returned to Mr. Q's classroom in a new set of dry, ill-fitting—and even worse-*smelling*—clothes that the nurse had pulled from the lost-and-found, their first class period was already nearly over. When the recess bell rang, Mr. Q told Brennan to hang back and dry the classroom floor, then he handed him a stack of brown paper towels as thin and absorbent as Bible pages. And his task wasn't just to clean the entrance that he sullied on his arrival, but everywhere else that his classmates had tracked their mud and water across the floor as well.

He had only managed to complete about half of his chore before the next bell rang, concluding his recess break. He stood up to return to his seat, but Mr. Q motioned for him to stay down, asking that he keep drying until nearly everyone had arrived—just so he didn't lose his momentum.

Brennan pushed those cold gray puddles around with his useless brown wads as more and more kids ran past him—one of whom bumped into him, knocking him down into a shallow puddle and slicking his oversized shirt all down his back like a chilly second skin. Still, he picked himself up and kept mopping up what he could until Mr. Q finally rose from his desk to the head of the class, presenting them with their writing prompt for the day—failing to offer Brennan as much as a word or a gesture to dismiss him from his chore, and then eyeing the boy with irritation as he scurried past the man back to his seat.

Once sat, he turned back to look at the new kid, etching the boy's soft, rounded facial features into his memory, so he wouldn't forget what he looked like come lunchtime.

During their writing period, Brennan could not bring himself to focus on his work—nor did he particularly care. He was far more focused on all of the different things he wanted to say to *that stupid little kid who thinks he's* so *smart.* What could he say to make him admit he was lying? What could he say to get him to stop? What could he say that might hurt the kid's feelings?

—   —   —   —   —

When the lunch bell rang, Brennan didn't stick around to see if Mr. Q had any additional cleaning tasks for him. He stuffed his backpack into his cubby and bolted for the door, clutching the excess waistline of his borrowed sweatpants through his ratty shirt just to keep them from falling around his ankles. His soggy shoes squeaked and squelched with every step down the hallway, and to the boy, each stinging, frozen step sounded like his shoes were laughing at him. Laughing at his pain. Laughing at what a dummy he must be to still think he was still a good boy. And soon, other kids would hear his laughing shoes and start laughing themselves.

But as soon as the first couple doors swung open and the hall filled with the white noise of grade school commotion, the sounds of his shoes were already impossible to pinpoint and, ultimately, drowned out in the noise.

Outside, Brennan was surprised to find that hardly anybody else had come out to the playground, then he heard the rain hammering down on the corrugated metal shelter above him, and figured everybody was probably holed up inside, keeping dry. He followed along the cover of the shelter to get a better view of the yard—past the long row of silvery metal benches along the brick wall, where, most days, the younger kids playing outside would all have to line up at the end of their breaks to be escorted back inside, single-file, by their teacher—but once he reached the end of the shelter, he still couldn't find his target, or anyone else, out by the jungle gym or the field either.

He ran back inside, then down the hallway to the cafeteria and lunch room, but after scanning the lunchline and the rows of faces sitting elbow-to-elbow alongside each other, his search for the new kid still turned up short.

94

He *knew* he had seen him in class earlier.

Did he get picked up early or something?

Or maybe, he thought, as a sly smile crept across his face, *Mr. Q asked* him *to stay behind and push water around with handfuls of scratchy paper?*

If that was the case, there was no way Brennan was going back to his classroom to check—not until the bell rang, at least—as he was certain that the mere sight of him would be enough of an excuse for Mr. Q to keep him after school again. But he still had to find where that little new kid was hiding, and set him straight before he could make any more kids sad with his lies.

He decided to make one more pass outside—even though he could still hear the rain pelting the shelter's roof from down the hall—and if the new kid wasn't out there, then he would turn back and head the other direction down the hallway, and check to see if maybe he was in...

The gym! Of course! That's probably where everyone who's not in the lunchroom went... If he's not outside this time, then he'll be in there for sure... The thought shot to the top of his mind as fast and attention-grabbing as a firework, nearly making him turn around on the spot, even as he pressed his hands against the door's pressure latch, allowing the door—with some help from the outside wind—to fly out of his grasp and blow wide open in an instant, the force of the howling gusts outside nearly blowing him back into the school. Once through the doorway, the winds didn't push him quite as hard, but he found that the door was now held open by some little brass fixture embedded in the concrete. He gave the door a tug to close it, but whatever held the door open, wouldn't let it budge.

He shrugged at the stuck door—figuring that, if he couldn't manage to budge it, then for sure an adult would eventually come by and close it—then he turned and squinted up at the big sycamore tree on the hill, but he still couldn't see anybody over there.

Even sheltered from the rain, the icy winds whipped at him, stinging his face, ears, arms, and hands, pushing and pulling him around by his baggy, billowing clothes. He was ready to skip his second search of the jungle gym and field, and head straight inside for the gymnasium instead—but that's when he saw him.

Down at the last bench, far along the sheltered brick wall, the new kid sat alone, cross-legged, with his eyes closed. The water hammered down, making a cascade of tinkling sounds with each drop that struck the end of the metal bench, just inches away from drenching his right side—though dark blotchy patches had already started filling in much of the right thigh and knee of his jeans.

Brennan's heartbeat jackhammered away at his thoughts. All along that sheltered path, passing bench after bench to his right, while the pouring rain to his left rivaled the volume and intensity of the anxious, driving noise in his head. It was the same rapid pounding that he felt whenever he heard the raised voice of his father or Mr. Q. But the feeling didn't make any sense to him this time. He wasn't in any *trouble*, and he certainly wasn't *afraid* of the new little pipsqueak. And while that hot, prickly feeling coursing through his body carried all of those familiar sensations in his chest and his head, there was something distinctly different—however similar—about this particular feeling.

Maybe, he thought to himself, *I just never felt this* angry *before? I guess nobody else ever* made me *feel this angry before.*

The thought made a lot of sense to him, and he started repeating it to himself—silent, but still mouthing the words, biting down hard on the word '*ever*', over and over: *No one's* ever *made me* this *angry before...*

If the new kid had looked up and watched as Brennan approached, he might have assumed that the older boy was talking to himself due to some mental or emotional disturbance— which, of course, Brennan *was* 'disturbed and talking to himself', but not in quite the same way that the new kid might have thought.

When Brennan reached him, he stopped a few feet ahead of his target, his lungs working overtime as he bobbed his head, psyching himself up for their talk, but the new kid hadn't even seemed to notice his arrival. He just sat with his eyes closed and a small, peaceful curve on his lips, as motionless as a CPR training dummy. His various lunch containers all stood neatly stacked next to his school bag, on the dry side of the bench—all empty, except for some leftover hummus.

Brennan tried out a few different poses while he waited for the kid to notice he was there. First, his hands on his hips, the way he had seen his father and Mr. Q do many times before, but something about it didn't feel right to him, and letting his arms dangle loose by his sides felt weird as well, so he settled on crossing his arms over his chest—which was his mother's usual posture with him when she meant business—and when he tried it on, it just felt *right.* He felt like *he* meant business.

"*Hey...*" Brennan said, his voice a dry croak, sounding like, '*Ehh*'—not even registering as a whisper in all that noise—so he cleared his throat and tried again, louder, saying, "Hey, uhh... *Kid.*"

The new kid blinked his eyes open and squinted up at Brennan. "Oh, *hi,*" he said, his peaceful smile brightening into a full-on beam at the sight of his classmate. "It's, uhh... *Wait— don't tell me, don't tell me...* It's... *Brennan,* right? Boy, I really didn't think anyone else'd be crazy enough to be out here in... You know, all of *this.*" He swung his right arm out in a wide swipe, gesturing out to the storm, and brought it back sopping wet. He gave the hand a couple of good shakes before wiping it off on his jeans with a laugh and a shrug.

The kid knew his name.

They hadn't even had a one-on-one conversation yet, and somehow, this new kid already knew Brennan's name. He couldn't recall the new kid's name if he had a hundred guesses.

Brennan was so jarred by the boy's greeting, he backed up a step without meaning to and had to catch himself. He could not have imagined receiving such a kind, friendly *hello*—perhaps the warmest he'd ever received—and especially not when he was so close to *laying down the law* on this kid.

He assumed the young boy would act more like... Well, '*bratty*,' he supposed. Or at least whatever '*mean liars*' were supposed to act like... He didn't like these new thoughts buzzing through his head. He didn't like the way they felt, the ways they confused him. He didn't like any of it.

Less than even a minute before, he felt so sure that he was doing the good, right thing ('*I must stand up to bullies and do the right thing—even when it's hard*,' *just like I pledged in assembly*, he kept telling himself), but now, the fire inside that was driving him forward had been suddenly doused by a new set of feelings. Everything he felt, felt bad—*wrong*, even. Like he had been tricked, somehow—or maybe even tricked *himself*—without realizing it.

But maybe *this* feeling was also part of it—part of what it's like to feel *really* mad at someone. The way grown-ups must feel when *they* get mad.

His foot started tapping at some point while standing there, but even once he noticed, he made no effort to stop it as he considered his next steps.

He rolled his shoulders back and straightened his posture, training his gaze on the new kid's face—the same stiff way he stood every time his father commanded him to, '*stand up straight and look me in the eye, when you're talking to me.*' He drew his mouth down low into a neutral frown, and let the muscles around his eyes all go slack, staring out at his younger peer from under a stiff brow.

"Where *were* you, new kid?" The words flew out of Brennan's mouth with more intensity than he had intended, the word '*were*' cracking into a shrill whine that screeched down the shelter toward the entrance, but the sound was snuffed out by the storm's noise before it could become an echo.

" '*Where*,' uhh...?" The new kid cocked his head back and twisted his mouth, initially dumbfounded by the question, then his face softened to a smile, and he asked in a calm, patient tone, "I-I'm sorry... Was... I supposed to *meet* you somewhere, Brennan? 'Cause I don't remem—"

"—I came out here before, at the start of lunch, but you weren't here. So where *were* you?"

"Oh. Well. I've pretty much been out here the whole time. I did go to the bathroom after class, before coming out here, but that's it."

Oh. The bathroom. He hadn't even considered that.

When Brennan didn't respond, the new kid continued, saying, "I mean, it was great to meet you all and everything, but—well, believe it or not, I don't *usually* socialize as much as I did yesterday with you all. Nothing against you guys; I just like spending time by myself."

Brennan gasped out loud at what he had just heard, and covered his gaping mouth with his hand, as though the new kid had just casually dropped one of the *really* bad words. Then he lowered his head, glowering down into the new kid's face as a fresh heat rose up within him, gathering in his face until his cheeks and forehead glowed a blotchy red. "My daddy *was* right about you! He was *right!* You really *are* a *socializer*—just like he said!"

"*Uhh...* Wait, I'm sorry, you think I'm a... *Huh?* I'm sorry, but I... I don't know what you... I don't understand..."

"Just forget it. Never mind. Anyways..." Brennan turned away, closed his eyes, and sucked in a breath before continuing. "Look, I wanna talk to you about something."

"Oh, uh..." The new kid's smile faded a little, but he nodded. "Sure, what's up?"

Brennan wanted to remain calm, careful with his words so he wouldn't end up saying anything bad—but the swirl of thoughts and feelings flooding his mind and body with each thump of his heart, made organizing his thoughts about as easy as trying to do his homework out in the middle of that rain storm. He hugged his arms tighter to his chest, then raised his head to look the kid in the eye. "Well, yesterday, you were talking about how your parents never hit you. That they just talk to you and help you with all your problems."

The new kid nodded again, his expression neutral but attentive. "Yeah, uh-huh. That's right."

"Yeah, well, I think that's a bunch of *lies*," Brennan said, uncrossing his arms and throwing them down to his sides, his voice trembling, nearly cracking again. "You go around making everyone else feel bad that we get hit, just because you think you're so much better than us. But you're *not*. You're just a stupid liar."

The new kid's eyes widened at the accusation, but he let Brennan continue, uninterrupted.

"So... *Yeah*... And—and my parents also told me the *truth*, that if you don't get punished sometimes, you'll end up bad and stupid and everything, and probably even go to jail. So people like you are gonna end up just like all those other bad kids who get into trouble all the time and never learn anything. So, maybe you should just shut up and tell the truth already."

The new kid lowered his chin, nodding and taking his time before responding, trying to pick the right words and sensitive tone that could still express who he is and what he was thinking, without upsetting the older boy any further. "I'm sorry, Brennan, but I'm not lying. I know it might seem kinda weird or different to you and your friends—and I guess maybe even your parents, too—but my mom and dad really *do* believe that talking and understanding each other is better for us than hitting. They think it helps me learn and grow better. And I think so, too."

Brennan stretched his lips into a thin, angry smile—not unlike his father's—shaking his head and squinting his eyes in discomfort. "But that's... I'm sorry, but that's just crazy. That's not how it *works*. Like, how are you ever gonna learn *anything* if you never get punished for the times when you're bad? It just doesn't make any sense."

The new kid sighed, glancing down at his lunch containers, then reached over and began stacking them into his lunch bag, looking back up at Brennan as he worked. "I just... I don't know what to tell you, Brennan. I'm sorry. I guess it's just a different way of thinking about things. My parents don't think punishment is really the best way to learn. They don't think it works the way a lot of other grown-ups think it does. They think—and I do, too—that, if I understand *why* something is wrong, and how my actions might affect others, then I'll keep making good choices because I *want* to—because I like making other people happy and because I believe that good things happen when we treat others with loving kindness—not just 'cause I'm scared I'll get in *trouble* if I mess up."

Wave after wave of hot frustration rose up in Brennan's throat and armpits, scoffing over and over in a way that sounded like he was hyperventilating. "But, that—that's just so *stupid!* That's not even how it *works,* you *stupid-idiot!* Look, *my* parents tell me the *truth,* okay—the *real* truth about stuff that people don't want you to know—and *they* say that people are all really selfish and mean inside, and so *that's* why we all need to be punished—to keep us from being bad all the time. *What's* so hard to get about that?"

The new kid's eyes drooped and half his mouth sagged into a lop-sided frown while he considered Brennan's words. "Well... I'm sorry, Brennan, but... I don't agree with that. I don't believe that people are mostly just selfish and mean. I think we also have a lot of good in us, too. All of us. And if we can just focus on understanding each other, and helping each other out, then maybe we can bring out each other's good stuff more than our bad stuff. That's what I believe, anyway. And my parents, too."

Brennan's boiling frustrations finally bubbled over, and all ot once, he couldn't feel the cold anymore.

He took a step closer, positioning himself between the new kid and the entrance, squeezing his fists at his side. "You just—*UGH!*—you think you're so smart, don't you? Huh? Just 'cause you skipped a grade, you think you know everything. Well, you don't. You're just a dumb, stupid, idiot *liar.*" His voice was loud now, drawing the attention of a few kids who heard the yelling from the hallway and wandered outside to see what the commotion was about.

The new kid zipped his bag closed and stood, looping a strap onto one shoulder and holding his hands out in a pacifying gesture. "Brennan, look, I'm sorry, okay. I'm really not trying to make you feel bad. I just want to help you understand. Hitting kids, or yelling at them, as a kind of punishment, is *not* okay. It's *not* normal. Even if every kid you'd ever met got hit, it would still be *wrong*. And it is *not* the best way to teach us how to be happy, healthy people who also want other people to be happy—no matter what you, or your parents, or anyone else thinks! And I just don't get how you can think that getting *whipped with a belt* is ever a *normal* thing to do to a kid, because to *me*, that's just—"

"—You shut up!" Brennan shoved the new kid hard in the chest, and watched as he stumbled back a couple of steps, out from the shelter and into the pouring storm, before catching himself on his back foot.

The curious group of kids who had come out to investigate the noise had already grown much larger as more and more students kept filing outside to see what was going on. Little by little, they all migrated their way down toward the two boys at the end of the shelter, trying to catch the action up close. But when they saw Brennan shove the new kid out into the rain, they all raced toward them, breaking into fist-pumping chants of, "*Fight! Fight! Fight! Fight! Fight!*"

The new kid peeled the slick hair from his eyes, tucking it back behind his ears, and looked up at Brennan with wide, pleading eyes. "Brennan, *c'mon! Stop it!* What are you *doing* right now? We don't have to do this! *Please! Stop!* I don't want to fight you!"

But Brennan wasn't listening. He stomped out into the rain to meet the kid, the wind flapping his soaked and billowing shirt around in front of him like a backward superhero cape. "I said… Shut *up!*" Then he raised his hands to the new kid's shoulders and shoved him back again, this push even harder than the first.

The new kid stumbled back another few steps, stopping himself just short of stepping back into an ankle-deep pothole that the storm had filled into a dense mud puddle. He advanced in a wide circle around Brennan, putting some distance between himself and the mud-filled hole while making his way back toward the entrance, raising his hands once more.

"Come *on*, Brennan—stop this! We're gonna get in *trouble!*" He had to shout to be heard over the relentless hollering of the wind, the rain, and the chorus of voices, all chanting, '*Fight! Fight! Fight!...*' "I don't wanna fight! Just stay back and... I don't know... *Cool off...* Talk about it later or something... *Please!* I don't wanna hurt you!"

But Brennan was finished talking. He didn't know exactly how this would play out, but he was determined to keep pressuring this kid until he gave up and admitted what a liar he was—and Brennan knew that he wouldn't be able to do that with his words alone. And now that there were other kids around, he'd have witnesses. They'd *all* hear the new kid's confession, admitting out loud that his parents really *do* hit him, and that he doesn't *actually* know right-from-wrong—like *regular* kids do—because his '*Socializer*' parents got him all mixed up and crazy, and that he just lied to everyone so that he could keep tricking people into liking him more and thinking he's smart. But nobody's gonna like him at *all* once they learn the truth.

The wrath coursing through Brennan's body felt like those first few seconds of breathing after seeing how long he could hold his breath, making him a little light-headed while his face and heaving chest throbbed with prickly warmth. Those feelings warped his eyes, nose, and mouth into ugly, strained shapes that they'd only ever made before when he was sobbing, but to the new kid, the older boy's twisted face looked nothing short of threatening.

Brennan lunged at the boy once more, his elbows cocked back, arms braced and his fingers spread wide, ready for the next shove—hoping *this* would be the one to knock the kid to the ground—but when he dug in his toes to launch himself at the new kid, thrusting his arms out with enough strength to topple any full-sized fifth-grader, his hands pushed nothing but air...

Because *this* time, the new kid was ready for him.

In a series of swift moves, he sprung forward at an angle toward Brennan's side, dodging the push while also catching the older boy's arm—grabbing his outer wrist with one hand and his elbow with the other—and then twisting those leverage points away from his body, while using Brennan's own size and momentum against him, leading him a few steps ahead where he could pin him harmlessly to the wet pavement until an adult arrived and he could explain the situation.

But after stumbling for only a couple of steps, Brennan's footing slipped and he twisted his ankle, sending him tripping and flailing his way out of the new kid's grip and diving face-first into the freezing, ankle-deep mud puddle.

The new kid leapt over to Brennan, grabbing the larger boy's arms just behind his wrists and dragging his face out of the puddle—submerging his lower half, from his belly button down to his knees, in the icy mud. Then, as soon as he could see that Brennan was able to breathe, he regained his hold on the older boy's wrist and elbow, pressing them into the concrete.

Brennan raised his head, squirming and jerking against the new kid's grip, and spitting out a bubbling mouthful of chunky brown water. "*Plah-puh! Ugh,* get *off'a* me! *Pluh!* Lemme *go!*"

"*No!* Not until you calm down, Brennan!" the new kid said, shouting back to be heard over the storm. His voice was firm, but not angry.

Above them, a terrible, ear-splitting klaxon rang out across the schoolyard—ringing loudest right above them, near the shelter—announcing the end of their lunch period, but neither boy acknowledged the sound.

Brennan continued wriggling around, his mud-caked face making him look like some kind of monster, barking to be released.

But the new kid ignored his commands and remained kneeling over the boy in silence, with one knee pressed gently against the pinned boy's ribs and the other reinforcing his grip on the outstretched arm. As the rain dripped down his face, guiding his hair back down in front of his eyes, he took the moment to slow his breathing down and collect himself while he waited for an adult to find them.

Then, a voice called out, "*Hey!*" from somewhere back by the sheltered area, no louder to the two boys' ears than a mosquito's *buzz* over all the surrounding noise. But moments later, the chanting abruptly ceased, followed by the rapid *kish-kish-kish* of splashing footsteps rushing up behind them, and they heard another voice—loud and husky, but definitely not the voice of an adult—saying, "Hey, get *off'a* him! What are you *thinking?!*"

Before either of them knew what was happening, a pair of hands thrust themselves into the new kid's armpits from behind, hoisting him up and off of Brennan, carrying him halfway back to the covered shelter as his heels dragged along the ground.

Brennan's heavy mud-soaked shirt sagged and dripped all down his front as he pressed himself up, out of the puddle, and onto a slouching seat on his heels, where he could finally scoop the mud out of his eyes with free hands. When he blinked his eyes open, he looked back and recognized his defender as the big sixth-grade girl with pigtails from the day before. But the girl paid no attention at all to Brennan. All of her attention and concern was directed squarely at the new kid.

She spun him around to face her, shaking him hard by the shoulders, saying, "Aw, you gotta be *kidding me*, new kid! I mean, come *on*—what were you even *thinking?* Like, yeah, I get it, these kids are *annoying* and all, but you never *start* a fight—not *ever!* That's how they *get* you—*everyone* knows *that!* Are you just *trying* to get in trouble, or what? ...Boy, I sure thought you was smarter than *this.*"

"But—well, *no*, I mean I—I just... I *didn't* start it. I even *tried* telling him that I didn't want to fight and that we were gonna get in trouble, but... But he just kept *pushing* me and *pushing* me... And I... And then I just..." The new kid's knees weakened, nearly dropping him on the spot, gasping and choking, before the big girl caught him, squeezing his arms together and shaking him again until he regained his composure. He glanced down at himself and found his clothes and arms all smeared and blotted with mud—though the rain had already rinsed off most of the biggest chunks. He turned up to face the big girl, the fresh tears in his eyes washing away with each blink, then back over at Brennan, sitting alone, caked in cold mud. "You *have* to believe me though, please. I really wasn't trying to hurt him—I *promise!*"

She shrugged and shook her head, baffled that he still wasn't *getting it.* "Yeah, okay, sure—but *who cares…?* I mean, yeah, *I* believe you, sure—but that's all *whatever* right now…" the big girl said, frowning down at the boy then picking the leaves and twigs off of him, and swiping off the remaining clumps of mud, "…I'm just saying, *good luck* explaining that to anyone who actually runs this school and expecting them to actually *care.* Naw, the way *they* see it: if you ever get yourself mixed up in a problem here, then you *are* the problem, boy. Don't even matter whose *'fault'* it is. Now, come on, let's hurry and get you outta here and cleaned up before someone—"

Her words were cut off by the ear-splitting trill of a whistle cutting through the storm, and a hoarse voice that definitely belonged to an adult—a woman—saying, "Alright, lookie-loos, y'all need to be heading on back to your classes… Go on, now… And as for *you two*, big, bad brawlers… Y'all li'l dummies really couldn't work it out with your *words?* You just *had* to start your little mud-wrestling match like a couple'a barnyard piggies? What were you kids even doin' out in this mess in the *first* place?" She scoffed with a sound like, *'pisshh,'* and said, "Alright, chuckleheads, I want both'a y'all, *inside*, with me. Let's go."

She walked past the big girl and the new kid, pursing her lips and shaking her head down at him as she passed them by, over to where Brennan was still kneeling next to the puddle, calling back over her shoulder, "And I want you waiting right there for me while I go and get your friend, new kid—and don't you even *think* about trying to run off now, or you'll make it ten-times worse on yourself."

The big girl left the new kid where he stood and ran up to the woman, tapping the side of her arm until she got her attention. "Hey… Hey, miss… That new kid—I was here, and I saw the whole thing go down, and I just wanna say, he didn't even *do* nothing—it was that other kid that started it! The new kid was just tryin'a—"

"*Girl,* I got enough going on here, and if you aint directly *involved* in this here fight, then I don't even wanna see your face around here right now—you *feel* me? So why don't you go on, get back inside now, back to your class, before I end up dragging all *three* of you li'l punks down the office? That sound good?"

"...Yeah, yeah," the pigtailed girl said, dropping her face at an angle away from the woman so she could scoff and scowl without them coming off as *direct* disrespect. Then she raised her hand, offering the new kid a stiff, *'so long'* wave and a sympathetic frown, and turned back toward the school, carving an easy path through the lingering onlookers with a few swipes of her arms, knocking them aside and into each other as she passed.

The playground attendant then turned her back on the retreating girl and, bracing one hand just above her knee and grunting in pain as she crouched halfway to the ground, she reached down and grabbed a handful of Brennan's shirt-scruff, right between his shoulder blades—where it was still soaked, but not muddy—squeezing it hard, like she was wringing out a damp rag with one hand. "Come on now... *U-u-up* you get!" she said, her voice straining as she hoisted him up and onto his feet with a single powerful yank.

Brennan was so jarred by the sudden shift to standing upright that his arms fell ragdoll limp by his sides, and the moment his soggy shoes landed with a *squish* on the pavement, his baggy, borrowed sweatpants dropped—*splat*—becoming a muddy wad around his ankles.

His legs and feet were so numb—except for the constant sting of the cold, nipping away at him like a colony of angry fire ants—that he didn't actually feel the rain and the breeze against his legs until *after* he heard the whooping laughter of the kids still gathered in the shelter behind them.

"*Uh-oh!*" came a voice from one of the onlooking children in a high sing-song. "Looks like *someone* had a little *acc-i-dent...*"

"Hey, *Bren-nan!*" called another voice, "Is that *mud* on your *chonis*, or did you just *caca* your pants because you're in trouble *again?*" Which only multiplied their roars of laughter.

When the playground attendant heard them, she whipped her head around and caught sight of a half-dozen or so stragglers, still peeping from the edge of the shelter, all pointing and laughing at them. She looked back down at the scrawny boy suspended in her grip, and in that moment, they both made the same startling discovery.

Brennan could only dangle there like a marionette on his tiptoes, stretching his hands down in front of him, trying to cover up his mud-speckled tighty-whities.

"Aw, *hell* no," she said out loud to no one in particular, her curse sounding like she'd said the word *'hail'* instead, then she spun on her heel to face the onlookers—wheeling Brennan around by his scruff in the process. "*Naw, nuh-uh!* The *bell* has *rung*, babies. What, you think I can't *see* y'alls' snickering li'l faces over there? Yeah, *go ahead*—keep laughing-it-up, ya li'l punks! You all laughing now, but you won't *be* laughing when I'm marching a whole *parade* of y'all down to the principal's office!"

She glared at the group as they casually drifted apart, expressing their sudden boredom with the scene via scoffing laughter and a few rebellious parting gestures, before sauntering their way back inside.

"*Pssh*—yeah, that's what I *thought...*" she said to herself, then shouted after them, "Yeah, y'all punks better *scurry* them li'l heinies back to y'alls' classes now—and I'm talking *double-time!*" But they were already well out of hearing range by that point.

Once the onlookers were gone, she looked down once more at Brennan, still swaying on his tiptoes in her grip. She released her hold of the boy enough to lower him back down to his heels, and with an exasperated huff, she said, "*Wha*—come on now—pull up your dang *drawers*, boy! What's the *matter* with you? ...Lord, who is even *raising* these children...?"

As soon as Brennan was back on his feet, he collapsed

straight down to his heels, setting his hands to work, busily scrounging and clawing his way through the dense, mud-slopped wads of freezing fabric as he searched for the waistband. The second he found it, gripping the sides between his thumbs and forefingers, he shot back up to his feet, hiking the ruined sweatpants up as high as they would go—reaching just below his armpits—and held the loop of excess waistline pinned there, with both hands, against his chest.

The playground attendant stepped back so she could give the shivering boy a once-over, frowning at the dark filth coating his entire front, from shoes-to-forehead. She shook her head at him, clicking her cheek and saying, "*Tsk.* Just *look* at you... What a state... Well, *alright.* C'mon. Let's get on outta this mess and get you boys cleaned up," then she grabbed hold of Brennan's shirt-scruff once more, as well as the back of the new kid's collar, and began marching them both back under the sheltered entrance. "...Nasty day like this, and you're tellin' me *this here's* all the clothes you got with you today? Boy, I can't even imagine what on earth could have possessed you, or—God forbid—your *parents* to let you leave your house in—"

"*—These aren't even my clothes! These aren't my clo-o-othes!*" Brennan lashed out, wailing like a lunatic and flailing a free hand around, twisting pointlessly in her grasp like an animal caught in a snare, barking, "I don't even *know* whose clothes these are! Where are my clothes?! Give 'em to me! I *want* them—I want my *clo-o-othes!*"

The woman did a double-take and gave the boy a bewildered smirk, unsure exactly what he could have meant by those remarks, but she shrugged it off as just *another one of those weird things kids say sometimes.* "*Still* yourself, child! Just take a breath and chill, okay? Now, I'm sure they can get y'all's clothes worked out once we get to the office, but for now... I'm gonna need you two wiggle-worms to hold still and come with me."

And together, the three of them marched back into the school and down the long, echoing hallway toward the principal's office.

—   —   —   —   —

When they arrived at the office, the playground attendant explained the situation to the school secretary—as well as Brennan's strange remarks about his clothes—and she allowed him to use their staff restroom to change back into his clothes from that morning. When he fished them out of their trash bag, his pants, shirt, and sweaters were all still dripping wet, and there were no spare shoes or socks to help dry his frozen feet either—but at least these clothes weren't covered in mud.

By the time he had changed and returned from the restroom, the new kid's parents had already come by and picked him up, leaving him all alone with the ancient, owl-eyed secretary. Shortly after he sat down, she suffered a furious, phlegm-gagged coughing fit, and Brennan shot out of his chair in a panic, asking the woman if she was okay, if she was choking, and if she needed him to go find help, but less than a minute into it, she cleared her throat, groaned, and resumed her typing as though nothing at all had just happened. She looked up at Brennan, frozen petrified in place a few feet from his chair and holding his breath as he awaited confirmation that she was going to be okay. She nudged her massive spectacles back up the bridge of her nose with a knuckle, then squinted at him through a scrunched-up face, motioning him back to his seat with a little *pat-pat-pat* motion in the air, saying, "I *say*... You there... *Boy*... Just *what* do you think you are doing out of your seat, *hmm...?* Not *mischief*, I hope...?" She poked pale gray tongue, in and out, from the dry, sticky corners of her mouth like a reptile, gathering the moisture to keep speaking, then she continued, the words crackling and popping in her mouth like rice cereal, saying, "Now then... You be a *good* little boy and stay right there... *Quietly...* That is... Until either *I*, myself... Or another member of our staff... Are able to reach your—" and at that, she broke out into another red-faced fit, hacking straight into her computer screen while Brennan crept back to his seat. Once the fit had passed, she resumed her typing, apparently oblivious that she was in the middle of saying something to him just moments before.

From that second one on, her coughing spells felt to Brennan like a ticking time bomb; just a matter of minutes until she would be seized again, bursting into one after another. He winced at the labored sounds of her wheezing as she alternated, at tortoise's crawl, between typing, placing phone calls, and leaving short, droning voicemail messages—dreading which sticky breath would be the one to set her off next.

After several failed and repeated attempts to reach Brennan's parents by phone—and a few more of the secretary's nerve-racking coughing sessions—his father was the first to eventually cave and answer her call to his work number. Even from Brennan's chair across the office, the boy could hear his father's voice barking through the phone—no specific *words*, just the heat of the man's emotions.

Brennan waited, shivering in that hard plastic chair, for what felt like an eternity. The entire office silent, except for the secretary's clacking on her computer and the occasional electronic whir of pages being printed.

Finally, Brennan heard the office door swing wide open followed by a pair of fast-stomping footsteps, and before Brennan could even see who had entered, he already knew. If the cadence of the man's steps were not enough to give him away, then the signature intensity of his *angry-voice* took care of the rest—as it was just as recognizable to Brennan as the man's face—snapping, "*Where is he—where's that little—ah*, there *he is! You!* You stay *right there*—I *mean* it. *Oh*, you are in worse trouble than you can possibly imagine, young man. I'm talking a whole new *world* of pain for you, boy. Oh, you just *wait* til we get home..."

Nine.

As soon as they walked through the front door—before Brennan could even change into a dry set of clothes or wash the mud out of his hair—the father was already burning to carry out his son's punishment.

As he slipped off his belt, he told Brennan that he'd be standing for this one. So, standing there, teeth chattering and shivering from the cold—as well as from his own fear—he hunched over at the waist, arching his back so his head and torso curved over like a banana, holding his arms tight to his chest with his little fists clenched and trembling under his chin while he waited for the crack of the first lash.

And then it came, purging all the air from his lungs in an instant and setting his whole mind and body ablaze with pain.

His eyes bulged wide, then slammed shut, lining his lids with hot, stinging tears. His breathing leapt to the shallow rapid breaths of a rabbit that just heard the shot of a nearby hunter's rifle. He struggled to suck down his next ragged breath, but it was cut short by the next lash. Followed by another and another until he quickly lost count.

But Brennan didn't care.

From that first lash onward, the pain short-circuited his brain from forming or following any new train of thought throughout the rest of that beating. In place of thoughts, Brennan's mind had become host to a snarling pack of feral beasts, all barking and snapping and yelping the primal sounds of their rage and terror.

As bad as it hurt him—and his father certainly did what he could to make sure that *this lesson* would leave a lasting impression on the boy—somehow, the actual lashes *still* didn't seem to hurt quite as bad as he imagined they would have on the ride home, with his father screaming in his ear the whole time, driving too fast and swerving around cars while other drivers honked at him. And though his punishment was excruciating, the white-hot anger burning behind his clenched eyelids kept him from wailing or crying out as he had before—or making any other sound louder than a whimper or a muted, guttural, '*Ngh!*'—after each fresh jolt his father's belt sent tearing through his body.

Brennan's angry feelings remained with him throughout the ordeal—burning just as powerfully as they had when he woke up that morning, and when he saw that new kid on the bench at lunchtime, and then when those other kids laughed at him—and the longer he stayed focused on those feelings, the less and less he cared about his pain, until it all felt so small inside him, he could barely feel it at all.

He wasn't angry at his father for hurting him. He already understood the value of what was happening to him. He knew that he was bad. This pain was simply going to help make him stay good. Or if not *'good'* exactly, then at least *better* than he would be without it. After all, starting fights is something only *bad kids* do. Brennan already knew this. And he *still* started a fight anyway. So this is what has to happen for him to remember just how bad it is. Every shiny red welt or blueberry-colored bruise was another little reminder never to be bad again, and every lesson that remained on his body—from his mother's little *moon-marks* to the puffy pink stripes where his father's belt broke the skin—was one more reminder to *'stay good'* than the new kid would ever get.

At one point, between the lashes, something tapped Brennan lightly against the back of his clenched fist. When another tap came a moment later, he urged his eyes to flutter open and saw the wet shine of a fat droplet rolling down a trail down the back of his trembling fist. For the first moment he saw it, in his hazy awareness, he assumed it must have been sweat, as a thin layer coated his entire body, soaking into his already drenched clothes. Something about his crying didn't add up to him. He knew that kids cried when they were sad, and sometimes when they got hurt as well—and he had certainly done his share of crying both during, and after, disciplinary sessions in the past—but even through the blinding pain, this was the first punishment that didn't make him *feel* like crying. He couldn't find or feel any trace of those familiar sad feelings within him. All that was there was the combined heat of his emotional inferno mingled with the jolts of pain firing off like a lightning storm throughout all the nerves of his body.

His first thought, once he could think again, was: *Can people get so angry that it makes them cry?*

— — — — — —

After what seemed to Brennan like an especially long pause between lashes, his father finally dragged a shirtsleeve across his dripping forehead and, between panting breaths, he said, "Alright... You're done now... You can go on back to your room... And just... You just stay in there for a while... Think about what you did... *Comprendé...?* I just... I can't stand to look at your face right now..."

Brennan turned in his father's direction but kept his eyes trained on a random curl of carpet a couple inches in front of his father's shoes and nodded his head. His face was a hard, red mask of blotchy skin stretched tight over clenched muscles, burning just as hot as his throbbing backside. His forehead was still dotted with sweat, his cheeks and chin smeared wet with tears, slick and glistening in the late-afternoon sunlight streaming through the window.

He turned, ready to once more limp his tortured carcass down the long hallway to his room, but after taking a single step, he was frozen in place by the sound of his father clearing his throat, "*Ah-hmm!*"

Brennan shuffled his feet, turning to face his father's direction, as slowly as an oscillating fan, without his gaze ever leaving the floor, though he could still see the man threading his belt back the loops in his trousers in his peripheral vision.

"I think you're forgetting something there, boy…" the father said, buckling his belt and crossing his arms.

Brennan remained perfectly still, uncertain of exactly what he could have forgotten, and too exhausted to guess.

When no response came, his father added, "…See, because, just now, I told you that we were all done here and that you could go back to your room—but you must not have heard me real good, 'cause I didn't hear you say a *peep* to acknowledge that you heard your old man."

Brennan gulped down a shaky breath. "Oh. *Uh…* Yes. Sir. *Sorry*, sir."

He turned away, looking as limp and lifeless as a plush animal with all of its stuffing pulled out, wincing as he advanced a step toward the hall before his father's voice halted him once more.

"*Mm*—nothing *else?* Nothing you'd wanna say to the man who had to abandon his work and all of his clients in the middle of his shift, not to *mention* the better part of a day's pay, all just to drive back here and pick up *your* sorry hide from school? You really can't think of *anything else* you'd like to say to me for everything I sacrificed for you today?"

"*Err…*" Brennan grunted, trying to think of what else he could say to make this all be over as quickly as he possibly could, before it eventually dawned on him, and in a voice so low, he almost didn't recognize it as his own, he said, "*Thank you, sir.*"

"That's *better*," the father said, his shoulders lowering from his jawline until they settled back into place. "Alright. You can go now."

The boy nodded and shuffled away, leaning against the hallway wall and limping his way back to his room.

—   —   —   —   —

Brennan closed the door behind him and stripped out of his wet clothes—slowly, like he was peeling sticky bandages off his entire body—and changed straight into his pajamas.

He generally preferred to sleep on his back or on his sides, but he had to crawl his way, inch-by-agonizing-inch, onto his stomach just to lay down at all, as he could find no other posture that kept his shredded backside from shooting pain throughout his body every time he breathed. And even the simple movements of easing himself down from his crawling position to laying down on his bed, allowed the pain to gather and flare up even worse than it was while his father was still doling out the punishment. As soon as he was lying all the way flat, he buried his face in his hands and broke down, twisting and contorting his face into all of the shapes that his anguish could sculpt. He wailed until his lungs ached and burned. He thrust an elbow behind him, up toward the ceiling, held it up there for the length of an exhale and an inhale, then rammed his little fist down into his bedding. Then he raised it again and hammered it back down. Again and again.

The anger that he woke up with that morning had never found a calm moment to settle or die down throughout that entire dreadful day, and when combined with the pain that colored his every movement and breath, he could no longer imagine a world that existed outside of his own rage.

He thought about how, even if that new kid—*that stupid idiot, that mean, lying, future-criminal kid*—goes his whole life and never learns a *real* life-lesson about not starting fights—*even though that stupid new kid was* really *the one who started the fight first when he decided to tell his lies and make everyone feel bad*—Brennan still wished that the new kid would get hit anyway, just so *he'd* finally know what it's like for once.

He sobbed into his pillow, still punching his bed, muffling his cries while his tears soaked a damp mask into his pillowcase, making it even more difficult to catch his breath between the sobs.

He carried on like that for as long as he could, then he raised his punching hand up to rest near his pillow and turned his head to face it, panting as though he had just finished running PE laps. He drifted off to sleep quicker than the time his dentist gave him laughing gas, and as he faded out from consciousness, the same thought played over and over, like a mantra in his head:

It's not fair... It's not fair... It's not fair... It's just not fair...

—   —   —   —   —

The *POUND-POUND-POUND* of a flat hand slapping the door yanked Brennan out of his dark and dreamless sleep.

His eyelids were so heavy, he could barely open either eye more than a squint, and he struggled to hold them both open at the same time. He wasn't sure how long he had been asleep, whether it was day or night time, or even what day it was. He looked at his alarm clock and its red LED face shone so bright, it burned the numbers *7:45* into his eyeballs. He blinked a few times, but even squeezing his eyes shut, he could still see the time lit up against the backs of his eyelids. He searched his brain for why somebody would be pounding on his door. A little light seeped in through his window, but it might look that way at 7:45 in the morning just as easily as 7:45 at night.

Did my alarm forget to go off? he thought. *Or did I... Sleep through it somehow...?*

Then, attempting to raise himself off the bed, he was sharply reminded of the punishment he received before going to sleep—as well as all the trouble at school before that. He had already experienced his dad's wrathful response to his fight with the new kid, but he had yet to hear anything back from his—

"*—Brennan?!* You better get your little hide *out* here, young man—*right* now! You are in for a world of trouble like you can't even *begin* to imagine. I already know about everything that happened with you at school today, and I am just *so, extremely,* disappointed in you, Brennan. I just don't know what's gotten into you these days. I swear, sometimes, it's like... Like I don't even know who you *are* anymore... Certainly not *my* good little beautiful boy... Because I *know* my son, and *my* sweet little boy could *never* do something as mean and horrible as... As... Well, *this*... And, sometimes, I think... It just feels like, one day, my good little boy just up-and-left—took off, out of the blue—and I don't even know where-in-the-world he ran off to... And *now*, we're just stuck with *you* in his place... Or like *you* just snuck in here and took over his *life* or something. I don't know... I just... I really can't tell you just how disappointed we are in you, Brennan... Anyway, you have one minute to meet me and your father in the dining room... And, um... Please don't keep us waiting... We're both already pretty maxed-out on our patience with you for the day..."

— — — — —

Brennan crawled backward off of the bed and onto his feet, dried his face off on his pajama sleeve, then opened the door and slumped his way back down the long hallway, ready to receive the second half of his punishment for the day.

Much like the punishment he received from his father, his mother's punishment wasn't even *half* as bad as he imagined it would be. It was mostly just her talking at him—much like she had when she came banging at his door—trying to find the perfect, soul-crushing combinations of words and emotional leverage points to make Brennan feel adequately ashamed of who he is. The only variety in her approach came in the form of a few sporadic bursts of shrill yelling—to ensure he was still listening to her—all while his father sat silently next to her, across from the boy, shaking his head and scowling down into his drink.

Brennan's face remained slack and emotionless throughout the ordeal, which only added more fuel to his mother's irritation and fury.

He had already heard most of his mother's talking points earlier at his door, but it seemed to Brennan like she just wanted to spend more time talking about how disappointed and ashamed of him she was, and how she didn't know who he was any more, and on and on. Sometimes she shouted her feelings, sometimes, she stated them in a detached calm. And other times, she whined her feelings through a sad and pleading mask—bearing all of the same anguished shapes and contours of a crying person's face, but with none of the actual tears.

For the most part, she cast Brennan as *The Problem* in her dramatic recounting of events—*What's the matter with you? What's wrong with you? What were you thinking?*—but there were a couple of occasions when she digressed, however briefly, into tangents casting herself as *The Problem—What could I have done? What* more *could I have done? Do I not do enough? Have I not sacrificed* enough *yet for you, for this family?!*—before dismissing the idea entirely and redirecting the blame back toward one of the other two present.

Once she had exhausted herself, she took a drink from her glass and said, "Well... All I can say is, I sure hope that, after all that, you have something good to say for yourself..."

Brennan shrugged, his eyes cast down at his vacant place setting—thinking back to just the night before, when they were all in *pretty much* good moods, laughing, eating, and having fun together.

When his mother's mouth dropped open and let out an insulted little gasp in response, he realized his faux pas, straightening his back, rising a full inch or two taller in his seat, and then, in a mumbly, monotone voice, as deep as his young voice could go, he said, "*Oh...* Uh... I mean, *I'm sorry*. And... Uhh... *Thank you?*"

At this, his mother scoffed and leaned way back in her seat, her mouth still hanging open, flabbergasted, but her eyebrows crinkled together now, glaring at him in shock as though he had just called her some unspeakably offensive name.

"Oh... *Sorry? Thank you? That's* the best you got? God, do you just think I'm *stupid,* or what? I mean, *seriously*—you think you can do something like this—go around bullying younger kids, picking fights at school, talking back to your teacher, being disrespectful to your parents, and then—*what* exactly? You just wriggle your wormy way out of trouble with a little *'sorry-thank-you, sorry-thank-you,'* sad-boy routine?"

She repeated Brennan's phrase back to him in an ugly, mocking tone, as though her mouth had difficulty forming the word-sounds, which—along with some jerky gestures of her hands for vulgar emphasis—made Brennan feel like she was not only making fun of him, but also suggesting that he lived with a mental disability that he knew nothing about.

"*No*, nah-ah. I don't think so, kiddo. Not this time. You've done the crime, so you are gonna do the time, mister, or so help me…"

Brennan's face flooded with a dizzying heat, and in an instant, all of his sadness and shame felt like it flushed right out of him, as all of his features leapt into sharp, warping angles, he peeled his lips back tight over his teeth and launched up from his seat, banging his ribs against the table as he rose, hard enough to slosh his parents' drinks around in their glasses, but he didn't feel it, or even notice the impact. He brought his little fists down on the table like a pair of *Nerf* hammers—not hitting it too hard, but still hard enough to rattle their drinks again.

In a matter of seconds, Brennan went from feeling like like he could have passed out right there at the table without a moment's notice to feeling like he could pick that entire table up above his head and snap it in half as easy as a cracker, just to see the looks on his parents' faces and watch them tremble at his feet.

"Th-then *what—huh?!*" The boy faced down his mother, jutting his jaw and glaring through her with sharp, scrutinizing eyes that chilled her blood on-sight. While she couldn't describe the experience—as she was hardly aware she was even experiencing it at all—there was some quality to the look on her son's face that evoked vague images in her mind's eye—little more than flashes and impressions, really—of all the 'angry grown-up' faces she had encountered when she was still a little girl, herself, and for just a split-second, she felt suddenly terrified of her son in a way she couldn't process. "What's the *right* thing to say? Wh-what do you *want* me to say? *Huh?* What am I *supposed* to say here? Y-y-you just want me to say that I *love* that stupid, lying new kid, and that it was only an *accident* that I tried to beat him up? You want me to go and tell him, '*Aw, I'm so sorry*,' all over again? The office people already made me say it once, but I don't care. I'll do it again, if I have to. It's stupid, and it doesn't even mean anything anyway, so I don't care if I have to apologize a thousand times... O-o-or do you want me to say that I *still* hate him because he's a stupid liar and a radical *Socializer*, just like you guys told me about—only I guess *I'm* not supposed to, like, actually *say* anything or *do* anything to make him stop...? O-or do you guys want me to say that I hate both of *you, huh?* A-a-and that I wish that we didn't even *have* this stupid family that's always yelling and saying mean stuff to each other, pretending like you're joking—only it never actually *feels* like you're joking—it just feels like you guys really *do* hate each other. *And* me. O-or maybe—maybe you guys just want me to keep hating myself the same way you guys hate me. Well, I probably *do* already. I hate myself a lot—*okay?* Just so, *so* much, every day. An-and whenever I get in trouble, and *trouble*, and *trouble* like this, I just wish, wish, *wish* that I was dead already so that I wouldn't have to keep getting in trouble all the time and getting yelled at all the time—so, is *that* good? Is *that* what I'm supposed to say?"

The mother held a trembling hand out inches in front of her face, then cupped it over her mouth as she sniffed back hard and her eyes filled with tears. "I-I can't—I don't... I don't even know what to say, I-I just... Oh, Brennan, sweetie... All I wanted... I just wanted you to tell us that you weren't going to do this again... I-I didn't think that you would... That you would..." Her voice broke and she gasped as her face erupted into wailing sobs. She slapped both hands over her mouth and ducked her head down into her lap, as though stricken by the sudden urge to throw up.

Brennan eased the tension in his shoulders, lowering them back down, but remained standing at the table as the weight of his head wilted his neck, dragging his gaze, once more, down to his empty place at the table. "*Oh.* Uh... Then... I guess I'm sorry about that, too... And, yeah... I, uh... I mean, I probably *won't*, you know... Do any more fights at school again... Stuff like that... I think I learned my lesson already..."

When she raised her head back into his view, gasping, sputtering, and sniffing between shallow breaths, his mother's face looked like it was melting, her eyes just two bloodshot, sagging slits floating in the inky darkness of their sockets. Her crying had given her a racoon-mask of dark, dribbling make-up, all smudged and staining a watercolor trail down the middle of her face, past her trembling, rubbery frown, and dripping little black dots from her chin. She shook her head over and over—more in response to her own thoughts and feelings than any words Brennan had actually said—and kept swiping at her eyes with rapid smears of the heels of her hands, like a rodent washing its face with its paws. Then she reached a shaking hand out to pick up her drink and, clutching it in both hands, she rose up out of her seat and shuffled a few steps away, mumbling, "*I... Sorry... I-I just... I'm sorry...*"—though it was unclear to the other two whether she was talking to them or to herself—before lumbering the rest of her way down the hall to her bedroom, slow, hunched over, and shaking all over, as though she were a much older woman.

The father then snatched his own drink up to his mouth, dropping it back down on the tabletop with a crack as loud as a home run hit. "God*dammit*, boy! *Unacceptable.* Did you really learn *nothing* from earlier?! That is *no* kinda way for you to talk to your mother—not *now*, not *ever*—do you *comprendé* me?"

"Yes, sir."

"I didn't hear that—*do you understand me?!*"

"*Yes, sir!* Stop *yelling,* please!"

"That's *better*... Now, I don't know what we're gonna have to do to get you back on the right track and have you stop acting like a jack-ass every time you get yourself worked up over something, and as of right now, I *still* can't stand the sight of you... But I can tell you one thing for sure... Your school told us they suspended you for the rest of the week on account of your little stunt today, but just 'cause you don't have to go to school for the week doesn't mean you've earned yourself some free vacation-time. It's gonna be at-home boot-camp for you, boy, which means that, for the next six days—and quite possibly, *longer*, we'll see—you'll be waking up early every morning, running laps, doing jumping jacks, push-ups, the whole deal. Then, you're gonna go through, pick through, sort through, and clean out that landslide-of-crap you call a bedroom. And after *that...* Well, I'm sure we can find some other chores to keep you busy and out of trouble. Point is, by the time next Monday rolls around, you will be *begging* me to go back to school... Anyway, that about does it for now... You go on, get back to your room. Get out of here. I don't want to see you again for the rest of the night."

"...Yes, sir. Thank you, sir." Brennan's face felt numb and paralyzed, like he was wearing some oversized Halloween mask in place of his actual skin.

Even though his stomach ached and grumbled, he knew better than to mention the fact that he hadn't eaten dinner yet, and didn't eat anything at school that day, either. The only thing he would get for that is more trouble. So, when the father dismissed him with a couple sweeps of his hand and went back to staring down into his drink, Brennan shrugged, turned in place, and slumped away, dragging his feet along the floor like a zombie all the way back down the hall.

Ten.

That next week did not play out quite the way the father had described.

Granted, the next morning—Wednesday—his father did take him out to the garage to teach him the proper way to do a push-up. Brennan understood what his father showed him, *in theory*, but he lacked the upper-body strength to do more than two in a row, even when his father showed him how to do the easy ones on his knees. Next, he had the boy do some sets of jumping jacks and jump rope, but the boy became exhausted after only a few minutes, at which point, they stopped and closed up the garage.

After that, they hopped in the father's truck and drove down to a local park, where he planned to have the boy run laps around the track, timing him from the bleachers to see how fast he could run a mile. It would have taken Brennan six laps for him to have completed his mile, but after only four laps—and after much pleading from Brennan, as his throbbing legs and lower-back were still screaming with pain from the day before—the boy eventually gagged and threw up on the track before staggering, stumbling, and collapsing into a heap, where he passed out.

—   —   —   —   —

When Brennan awoke, he was sitting upright, strapped to a soft seat, as cold air blasted him in the face. He heard the sound of the road rumbling by beneath them, then his father's voice cut through the disorienting haze of bright light all around them, saying, "*The-e-ere* you are, now... There he is... It's okay, buddy... You're alright now... Yeah, you're alright... C'mon, here, drink some more of this... It'll help... That's it... Nice and easy…"

Brennan sputtered and coughed up the stinging, acidic liquid in his mouth. "*Pluuh—what—?*"

"—It's *alright*… Take it easy… You just got a little overheated, is all. We just gotta cool you down some. Shoulda probably picked a better day to do this—maybe a nice overcast or something, but… Well, I guess now we know for next time. Anyway, here, just keep drinking more of this and it'll help cool you off quick. Here, take it—*take the can*—I'm tryin'a drive."

Brennan reached out and took the chilled red soda can from his father and pressed its lid to his mouth, slurping back gulp after gulp and gasping when he finally came back up for air.

"Hey, so, uh… You know, your mom's been having a pretty hard time lately with you getting in trouble and all, so I was just thinking… Maybe we don't even mention this whole thing that happened at the park, you know? 'Cause you know *her*—you know how she worries—and if she hears about how you… You know… How you got a little too hot back there, and started feeling woozy and everything… I think that kinda thing would just make her worry even more, ya know…? And after your little tantrum *last night*… Well, I just don't think you'd wanna say or do anything to make her worry even *more*—wouldn't you agree? I mean, especially since you're already feeling better again, right…?" He patted Brennan twice on the thigh. "…Isn't that right, buddy…? You feeling all better…? You definitely *look* a lot better, that's for sure…"

Brennan said nothing, but his eyes grew wide open in response, turning his head with an eerie slowness to face his father—like something he must have seen in a preview for a scary movie. The man kept doing double-takes at the creepy-eyed kid sitting next to him, growing increasingly unnerved by his son's unusual stillness while also trying to keep his eyes on the road.

"*Err…* You *okay* there, bud? That sound like a plan—what I just said? Keeping your little spill at the park back there between you and me? I just don't want her to worry any more than she already does—and I know you don't either, right?"

But still, no response came, and every time he glanced back over at Brennan, the boy was making bug-eyed, unblinking eye-contact with him. Then the boy slowly raised his face toward the cab's ceiling, opening his mouth as big and wide as he possibly could, and he let out a bellowing burp that went uninterrupted for the full length of a slow exhale. When he finished, his gaping mouth was replaced by a squinting, toothy grin.

"Whoa-ho-ho! *Okay!*" The father laughed, more relieved than humored by the burp itself. "So, does that mean it sounds like a plan then?"

Brennan nodded his head in reply, still beaming his cheesy grin, and giving his father a thumbs up.

"*There's* a good man. Now, what do you say you take the rest of the day off and we go grab us some ice cream before I gotta drop you off and head to work? Then tomorrow, we'll dive right back into our at-home boot-camp—how's that sound?"

—   —   —   —   —

Thursday afternoon, before leaving for work, the father escorted Brennan on trips back and forth between the house and the curb, talking at him the whole time, as the boy dragged their various waste bins out to the street for pick-up. He commanded that Brennan was to spend his entire day cleaning and organizing his room—"*and not just some half-assed, Mickey-Mouse job, either*"—and if he couldn't finish the project all in one day, then he would just have to keep at it, day after day, until it looked tidy and presentable.

"...And I'm gonna go ahead and call you here at the house on my lunch hour," he said, "just to make sure you're not outside smelling the flowers, or watching some dumb-assed show, or playing your little idiot-box games or something. Now, if it's anybody other than me or your mom on the other line, you can just go ahead and hang up—nobody but telemarketers and relatives call that line anyway—but when *I* call here later this afternoon, you had better pick up that phone. *Comprendé?"*

Brennan's father made it clear that he was not to play *any* video games or watch *any* TV until *after* his room was completely finished, *and* approved by his father—though he *could,* if he wanted, stream some music from one of the man's approved classic rock playlists while he cleaned.

The intensity of his father's order left Brennan feeling bewildered. The man had never complained about the state of his room before that week, and his bedroom never seemed particularly messy or cluttered to him—especially when compared to those of some other friends his age—but his father seemed firmly under the impression that the room was nothing short of a biohazardous waste dump.

Sure, he didn't *always* make his bed in the morning, and a few of the things scattered about the floor *could* be picked up and arranged to look a little nicer upon entering the room, and there *might* have been a shirt here, or a sock there, that didn't quite make it all the way into his laundry hamper—but he made sure that all of his wet clothes from Tuesday's storm made it in.

For nearly a year, by that point—ever since the explosive evening when his mother returned from a hard day and broke down, breathlessly venting at him as she outlined all of the little things in her life that weighed her down, or held her back from reaching her potential, and kept her feeling so drained and exhausted every day—Brennan remained diligent to help her out, in his own small way, by washing at least one load of his own clothes every week, as well as his bedding twice a month.

But as far as any 'mess' in his room… That was about it.

He never had what most people would consider, 'a lot of toys'. The only real *toys* he had around the room were the small menagerie of various stuffed creatures and characters, a chest full of his favorite action heroes, and a few decorative building-block playsets, fully-built and sitting atop the two-by-two cubby-shelf full of picture books he'd outgrown years ago. The vast majority of his bedroom entertainment came from one of his various screens. Whether he was watching shows or playing video games on his TV, or zoning out to videos on his tablet, he could keep himself amused for hours on end while making no bigger mess than the occasional tangle of charging cables.

He couldn't remember the last time his father had been in his room, and he wondered just what about it he thought was so messy. But, despite his confusion, Brennan agreed that he would spend the day cleaning it anyway, and as soon as his father left for his job, Brennan wasted no time getting to work.

First, he began by circling the room in stiff-jointed marching steps, imagining himself as a high-tech cleaning robot, gathering up every scrap of clothes he found that wasn't hung up or tucked away in a drawer, and then dumping them into his hamper with each pass, all while describing each of his actions out loud in a buzzing, monotone voice. Then, he did likewise with his stuffed friends, arranging them all neatly atop his chest of heroes. Next, he picked up his hamper, carrying it out in front of him to the laundry room, and started his load in the washer, *chirping* and *beeping* to himself the whole time.

He had an hour to kill, so, stumped on what he should do next, he figured he should head back to his room and make his bed while he waited to switch the laundry.

After making his bed, he returned to check on his load and found that it still had another fifty-three minutes remaining in its cycle.

Back in his room, he looked around for any *hint* of something that his father might deem *messy* when his TV caught his eye. He noticed that its usual black shine was looking more of a dark, dull beige. When he slid his finger along the screen, it cut a line of deep black through the filmy buildup, parting waves of gray-brown fluff in its wake. He inspected his finger and found a curled, wispy tangle snagged and dancing on his frayed nail. The fingertip itself was coated in a layer of gray powder that didn't come off right away when he rubbed it against his jeans—like the time he smushed a moth with his bare palm.

He ran to the bathroom and rinsed off his finger, then he unspooled a mound of toilet paper from its roll, tore it off, and carried it back to his room, bundled in his arms. He pulled a length of the paper out of its greater wad and pawed at the screen with it until its whole face looked as black as his earlier finger-streak—ultimately, using *far* less toilet paper than he had first estimated.

When he noticed the floaty bits of fluff swaying at the edges and corners of the screen, he wiped them clean as well, and kept wiping his way all along the sides and back until he had made it as far around the TV as his arms could reach.

Then he did the same for his gaming system and tablet—the former infinitely grimier than the latter—before flopping himself back onto his bed and letting his legs dangle off the edge. He couldn't think of anything else in his room to clean, but then he remembered his laundry. He hadn't heard the alarm go off yet, but it took him so long to wipe his stuff down, he was sure that the load must have finished its cycle by that point. And yet, when he went to check on it, he was dismayed to learn that the washer still had another twenty-six minutes left to go.

Even though he still didn't believe his room looked terribly *messy* before, he felt a rare swell of pride thinking about how it had never looked any cleaner than it did right then. But as good as his accomplishment felt, the feeling was short-lived, as he was still stumped on how he might occupy the rest of his day doing chores when he couldn't even think up a single other chore to do. There were no dishes in the kitchen sink for him to throw in the dishwasher, and nothing in the dishwasher to put back in the cupboards. He had already mowed and watered their lawn that previous weekend—and he wasn't about to start asking the neighbors about *their* yards unless his father brought it up again first. And even if he *wanted* to start on his homework, he left his school bag back in his classroom cubby and had no clue what books he was supposed to read and report on anyway, as Mr. Q hadn't passed out their weekly assignment sheets by the time Brennan was sent home.

Twenty-four minutes left.

He went back to his room and plopped down on his bed in

front of his TV, and before he could really think about what he was doing, the remote was already in his hand and he was thumbing the power button. "Oh, *shoot!*" he said, and turned the TV off again, forgetting for a moment that he wasn't allowed to watch anything or play any games until he finished *all* of his work.

But... Aren't I kinda finished already? he thought. *I mean, I still have to dry and fold and put away my laundry... But that's it. And I can't even do anything about it right now, anyway. I just gotta wait... But I did already clean a lot... And I'm pretty much done already... So... It'll probably be okay if I just watch a little bit. Besides, it's just enough time to finish an episode before the laundry's done.*

And so he did. He thumbed the TV back on, tapping his dangling toe as he set up the next episode of *Just The 3 Of Us*. His heart swelled as an automatic response to hearing those familiar opening notes of the theme song. He opened his mouth and drew in a breath to sing along, but this time, no sound came out, and he just remained staring at the show's opening montage with a twisted, almost *pained*, expression on his face, and still holding his breath. Something felt different about those opening images—a slideshow of the highest highs and lowest lows that the Aislingers have shared with their omniscient viewing audience, but still with varying degrees of smiles present in every clip—it all felt *off* to him somehow. *Phony.* It was all the same footage he had seen countless times before—and he knew that the show was make-believe anyway, and that they weren't even a real family, just actors who only pretended to love and care for each other so they could get money—but something about watching all their happy, smiling faces this time felt *extra* fake. Like they were *lying* to him. He remained silent throughout the theme song, panting rapidly through his nose after finally releasing his held breath, trying to shake his lingering thoughts and feelings, and settle himself into the episode.

Coincidentally enough, the episode he started—titled, "Brian's Fight"—involved the boy, Brian, getting dragged into a fight at school, after trying to defend a girl on the playground from two bullies who were trying to force-feed her some mushrooms they found growing in the schoolyard. Like Brennan, Brian got called into the principal's office (though Brian's principal was actually there to talk with him), and his parents had to come and pick him up, and at home, they similarly pelted him with questions like, '*What were you thinking, picking a fight at school?*' and '*What was going through your head?*'; but *unlike* Brennan, Brian's parents became concerned and stopped speaking once Brian broke down and started crying, actually listening to what he had to say.

Once he had explained the situation to them—that he was trying to help and protect someone else—then they immediately understood, apologized to him, and they both dropped down to their knees for a tearful family embrace, as the family reconciled this painful conflict together.

Just after the family's heartfelt huddle, while they were all huddled together on the couch, trying to figure out a plan for when he goes back to school, Brennan finally jammed the *power* button on the remote, blipping the Aislingers out of existence and flinging the remote down to the carpet. He stared hard at the blank screen, sounding like an old-timey train engine as he shot hot jets of air out of his nose.

The washer chime sounded from across the house. Brennan shot out one last huff, then he rose from his bed and went back to his work, switching his load to the dryer and starting the machine exactly the way his mother showed him—even remembering to throw in the sheet of that weird-smelling paper after loading all the clothes to make sure they came out feeling extra soft.

While the dryer did its thing, Brennan considered his options for lunch. There were no easy, finger-food leftovers like burgers or nuggets, leaving noodles as his only filling option, but he still wasn't *technically* allowed to bring sugary drinks, or any '*liquid-y*' foods in his room anymore—not since the time, back in second grade, when his dad had to spray his room down with ant poison, forcing Brennan to crash a few nights on the living room couch. But that was all back when he was still *little*, and he had learned to be much more careful with his food since then.

As he unwrapped its packaging, filled the styrofoam cup with water, and popped it in the microwave, he reassured himself that he could handle this one meal without making any messes and that all would be fine—just as long as he remembered to throw its empty cup away in the kitchen trash once he was finished. When the microwave dinged, he carried the hot cup back to his room, where he plopped back down on the edge of his bed and surfed through the options for a new show to start as he slurped away on his noodles.

He stumbled onto a cartoon series that caught his eye, called, *"Nuclear Fam,"* about an average American family called *"The Nablers"* that cracked Brennan up, just from its preview (even though he didn't quite grasp any of the jokes they were making, he found the *ways* they said things constantly hilarious). The father was an overweight idiot, who talked down to the rest of his family with haughty arrogance, even though it was clear that they *all* knew better than him—including the baby and talking dog. The slender mother, always speaking in a dull monotone as though she was constantly exhausted, was the beating heart of the Nabler family, doing her best to reign in her husband's outlandish plans, as well as cleaning up the messes after his epic failures—and all while clutching a seemingly unending glass of red wine every time she's on-screen. Generally, she had the patience of a bored saint, but every once in a while, when she got pushed too far, she would go berzerk, unloading a string of brutal insults until the person she told off shrunk in horror, before returning to her sweet, normal state. Unlike *Just The 3 of Us*, none of the children were near his age, but even though he didn't have a baby brother or an older teenage sister, he tried to imagine himself as the teenage boy in the show—though, this became harder and harder to do as the show went on, since the boy in the show was in high school, drove a car, and had a girlfriend. The Nablers, Brennan noticed, were much less kind and gentle with each other than the Aislingers, saying mean-yet-funny things to each other, while nobody ever seemed to cry or get their feelings hurt. In that first episode he caught, he even saw the father strangle his son after crashing his new car until the mother pulled him off of the boy, then began strangling him herself. But by the end of the episode, they had all made up and everyone was happy.

The theme song might not have been as catchy, or as fun to sing along to, as his old show, but Brennan liked how this new show made some dirtier, more *'grown-up'* jokes, and even dropped a few swear words that would surely land him in trouble if he had ever repeated them. More than anything, however, he liked how this show didn't make him feel like it was lying to him. If anything, it felt like the characters in this new were being honest like his parents were honest, casually talking about the kinds of *sad-but-true* things about the world that the people out there don't want him to know about.

When the dryer's alarm went off, he set about the same routine as before; setting his unfinished noodles down atop his bookshelf, pausing his episode, and then bounding across the house to the laundry room, gathering, folding, and putting away his laundry like he was training for the laundry Olympics.

Once he had finished his laundry, he returned to his episode, laughing so hard at one point, he choked on his noodles until his eyes watered and he had to cough them back into his cup. Once the episode finished, he powered up his gaming system, scooped a controller from its charging station, and crawled up the length of his bed before taking a reclined seat against his headboard, kicking back and logging in for his first extended gaming session in months—or at least since starting the fifth grade.

After a couple blissful hours of gaming, he heard a faint chime going off somewhere in the house—much quieter than the laundry alarm—and despite its familiarity, it took him a moment before recognizing the sound as the ringing of the house-phone. He paused his game and dashed down the hallway to the living room, snatching up the handset just as it was clicking over into voicemail.

"Uhh... *Hello...? Father-sir...?* Is that *you?*"

For the first few seconds, there came no response from the other end, no sound at all, then Brennan could make out the muffled wet slopping sounds of somebody chewing, open-mouthed, on the other end, before, finally, a familiar voice appeared, speaking between his bites and swallows. "Ah... *Good*... You picked up... How's the cleaning going?"

"*Oh, uh-h-h*... It's *going*... *Good*... Yeah, it's *good*."

"*Mm,* good... And you're not just wasting time playing on your idiot-box or watching TV, right?"

"*Huh-wha—? Me?* You wanna know if I was... *Oh*, like, if I was playing the, uh... On the, *erm*—oh, *no!* No, father-sir, I would *not* wanna waste my time on dumb stuff like that when I still have important stuff to do. I know better than *that*. That stuff's just for fun times—like, after all my chores and stuff are done."

"*Mm.* I see... Well, if *that's* really the case..." the father said, his voice trailing off into the monotonous churning sounds of his chewing.

Sudden sweat drops streaked icy lines all down Brennan's back, and he held his breath, anxiously awaiting whatever fate his father had in store for him at the end of the man's thought.

He was certain the man knew he was lying. Somehow, he *always* knew. Brennan didn't know *how*, exactly—whether his father was simply gifted with some lie-detecting sixth sense, or if Brennan himself just had some unknown *tell* that betrayed all of his attempts at dishonesty—but however it worked, the man always seemed to know whenever he was lying to him or leaving some little detail out of a story. And Brennan *also* knew that—as his father was always so quick to remind him—*the punishment'll always be worse if you lie to us about it.*

He felt so *stupid* for even trying to lie—and all for what? So he could eat lunch in his room and play some video games? No *way* was that worth whatever his punishment was going to be.

As the silent seconds stretched on, Brennan thought more and more about confessing being his best option at that point—just blurting it out before his father could call him on his deception, admitting that he actually *was* playing games, but that he's super sorry for lying about it, and how he thought it would be okay, but it was really just a stupid idea, and that he'll never, ever do it again—when suddenly, the staticky white noise of somebody slurping through a straw came crackling through the other end of the line, followed by the cascading sounds of, *Gulp-gulp-gulp... Ah-h-h-h...* Then the father cleared his throat and picked up from his previous dangling thought with a congratulatory flourish, saying, "...Then *good man!* And I couldn't be happier to hear you say that! It's nice seeing you turn your behavior around so quickly. You see what can happen once we get a little discipline in you? Guess all you really needed was a *father's* touch after all... You keep this up, and—if it looks like you made some real, honest-to-goodness progress on your room by the time I get back there—then maybe, *ju-u-ust maybe*, I'll bring home something *extra* special for dinner tonight... But that's only *if! Comprende?*"

Brennan stuck out his tongue and nodded his head, trying to make it flap around limp like a dog's—despite the fact that his father couldn't see him—and gave his response in a series of rapid, panting bursts, saying, "*Yeah! Yeah! Yeh-yeh-yeh-yeh-yeah! Yeah-yeah!*"

"Well, alright. Then you keep cleaning, and we'll see when I get home just what kind of dinner you'll be eating tonight... Anyway, I guess that's pretty much all I had to say for now, so... Back to it, I suppose—*chop-chop!*"

And before Brennan had the time or breath to say, '*buh-bye*', the line had already clicked over into dead silence. He had to briefly search the phone's face for the *End*-button—as he so rarely ever used the thing—before resting it back in its charging cradle. Then, he just stayed there for a while, glued to that spot, blank-faced and blinking at the phone, taking in the exchange and replaying what just happened on a loop in his mind.

Unless his father was only *pretending* not to know—which Brennan deemed 'unlikely,' as his father was always quick to point out anything he said or did not say as evidence to condemn him—then it seemed like he really did *believe* everything his son had just told him. Yet, what he told his father was *not* the truth—in fact, it was an outright *lie,* and lying, as he knew, was *bad...* But, what he said *also* made his father feel *good.* And *happy.* And *proud* of his son. And Brennan very much liked the way that all felt. And the best part of it all was that he was getting to do exactly what he wanted without getting into *any* trouble—at least, not in any *new* trouble.

He made his way back to his room, wondering what the night's special dinner treat could be, and with food on his mind, he grabbed the cup of cold, swollen noodles from his shelf, twisted his fork in the cup, and brought it up for one more big bite, before taking the rest of it to the kitchen and dumping everything but the fork in the trash.

After that, Brennan was free to spend the rest of the day lounging on his bed, saving the galaxy, and having the most fun he could remember.

—   —   —   —   —

His father was the first to arrive home from work that night, his arms wrapped around two large cardboard buckets of fried chicken, with a loaded plastic bag of sides dangling from one hand. Brennan stood frozen in front of him, his hands clasped low behind his back, head tilted downward toward his father, his eyes, once again, bulging wide open, and sucking both of his lips into his mouth, giving him an unsettling, too-tight grin that looked both half-goofy and half-ghoulish. After a beat of uncomfortable silence, the boy cracked his mouth like a baby bird opening up for whatever food its mother brought, his inward-curving lips serving as his beak, and he squawked, "*BAHP!*"

"Hey, what's going on, ya little weirdo? I sure hope you're hungry and didn't fill up on too much junk food, 'cause I just went and picked us up a whole *coopful* of chickens for dinner tonight."

Brennan rocked up and down on his toes, bouncing in place

while he squawked, "*BAHP-BAHP-BAAHHP!*"

"I… Guess I'll have to take that as a '*yes,*' then. The *real* question here is… Do you actually *deserve* this delicious feast? Because *this* chicken right here is only for good boys who cleaned their room like they were supposed to. Now… Does that describe *you?*"

With his lips still frozen in that uncanny grin, Brennan unclasped his hands from behind his back, raised a single finger up in front of his father, wiggling it like a stationary inch-worm, pointing the way down to his bedroom, playfully clucking, "*Bahp, bahp, bahp…*" in a coy sing-song.

The father laughed. "Well, *alright.* Finished it all in one day, huh? And you're sure you weren't just back there playing on the boob-tube?"

Icy needles pricked a frosty stripe all the way up Brennan's spine—and, for a few seconds there, he forgot how to breathe again—but he had to force himself to say *something,* or else his father would see through him for sure.

He licked his lips, glancing momentarily back down the hall toward his room, before snapping back to lock eyes with his father, shaking his head, and bleating, "*NA-AHP!*"

"Aw, good, great. Glad to hear it, bud. Then what do you say we go back there, huh? Check out the damage… See if it's up to regulation standards. You can go on now, lead the way…"

Brennan nodded his head low and stiff, as though bowing at the waist, then he bent his arms into an L-shape—hands out in front of him, palms facing each other—and pivoted on his heel, marching down the hallway, looking more like a tin soldier than an actual soldier—and making little *beeps* and mechanical whirring sounds with his mouth in sync with his movements.

When they arrived at the door, his father dropped a hand on the doorknob and sighed a deep exhale. "*Whoo…* Here we go, kid; the moment of truth… I really hope you're not wasting my time, son… I just don't know how much more disappointment I can take right now…"

Brennan's heart plummeted down into his guts. He relaxed the tight, creepy smile he'd been holding, allowing his mouth to slip back into its natural shape, and his wild-eyed stare dimmed into narrow, blinking slits as he did his best to take in the meaning of his father's words. Then, he let out a sharp sigh through his nose and perked his head back up, resuming his creepy-silly face and prodding the extended fingertips of both his hands into his father's ribs, motioning the man inside, and squealing, "Ee-e-e! *Ee-e-e-e-e!*"

His father laughed and raised his palms in surrender. "Hey, *alright, okay!* I mean, it's *your* funeral if the place is still a pigsty, but… If you say it's all finished…"

He opened the door, flicked on the light, and plodded his way to the middle of the room, resting his hands on his hips and getting his bearings while he waited for his eyes to adjust to the light. He swiveled back to look at the bed behind him, muttering, '*Mm… Bed's made at least, that's good…*', then, after kneeling himself down to the floor like he was about to do push-ups, he opened his phone's flashlight and looked under the bed, scanning the empty space from head-to-foot, but finding nothing under there bigger than a dust-bunny. He raised himself back up to standing, patted down the front of his shirt, and gave the bed a stiff nod before turning back to Brennan. "*Uhh…* Am I *missing* something here, bud, *or…?* Where'd you put all your stuff? I *hope* I'm not gonna find it all piled up in your closet, so when I open the door, I end up buried under an avalanche of your crap… I *won't*, will I?"

"Nope!" Brennan chirped, giggling, then he perked up and corrected himself, saying, "…I mean, *NA-A-A-ARP!*"

His father shook his head at his silly son and went for the closet door. When he clicked the light on inside—much like underneath Brennan's bed—he was astounded by how much empty space he found. The only things on the floor were three pairs of shoes pushed against the closet's back wall. Above those, just rows of his clothes all neatly hung on their racks, and then above *those*, sat some old board games, mementos, and a few other dusty knick-knacks that his parents had long-ago placed on that shelf for storage.

He clicked the light back off, closed the door behind him, and turned to face Brennan, scratching his chin. "*Oka-a-ay...* I gotta ask again... Am I just missing something here, or *where-on-earth* did you put all of your *stuff?*"

Brennan giggled again. "*Huh?* I don't really get what you mean? Like, it's all right *there*. Some of it's on that shelf, and some of it is in that big box, and some of it—like my plushies and stuff—is all just sitting right there on top. I guess I just don't really have a lotta stuff."

"Oh, come *on* now—that's a bunch of baloney, and you know it—you gotta have more stuff than *this*, right? I mean, this room is... It's practically *immaculate*... What about all of the loot you get from your birthdays and Christmas and stuff?"

"Well, I usually just want, like, gift cards and stuff. For games, mostly."

"I mean, sure, yeah, alright—but *still,* this still seems pretty..." His father paused then, squinting, then stalking around the corner of the bed toward something that caught his eye. "*Err...* What's the story with... All *that?*" He scrunched up his face and pointed a swirling finger at the mound of unused toilet paper on the floor next to his game console.

"Oh, that? That's just what I used to wipe the gunk off of the TV and stuff. But... I still have a ton of extra paper leftover. So, like... You guys can have it back if you want; just to use like normal, regular TP. There's nothing *wrong* with it."

"*Oh*, we *can*, can we? Gee, *thanks!* How *generous* of you!" The man laughed. "So, wait... Are you telling me right now that you actually *dusted* your room?"

"No, no..." Brennan said, shaking his head, "I didn't, like, actually *dust* anything. I just kinda wiped off all the little crud-fluffies."

"'*Crud-fluffies*', huh? Well, hate to break it to you, bud, but... That's exactly what '*dusting*' is. Just getting all that dust off."

"Yeah, but, like... My TV's not *that* old, and I didn't even have one of those *things*—you know, like, one of those *maid* things with the floofy tops?"

"I mean, you can call it whatever you wanna call it, but at the end of the day... Well, I just definitely wasn't expecting you to go and do all *that!* Oh, and just *wait* 'til your mother hears about this—'*but it wasn't* real *dusting!*—oh, boy, is she gonna crack up, I tell you. Well, I think this all *definitely* deserves some original recipe—wouldn't you say? Oh, hey, and, uh... Just so you know, son—and let's just keep this part between you and me—but, uh... *Dusting*... As far as *chores* go... Well, that's really more of a *lady's* job than a *man's* job. You know what I'm saying? Like, you don't really need to worry about stuff like that in the future. It's nice that you did it, and you're not in trouble or anything like that, but I'm just letting you know: you don't need to worry about the dusting from here out—*comprendé?* Lord knows, I already have to grin-and-bear-it every time I see you helping your mother with the laundry or the dishes, but... Anyway, that's enough of that... You ready for that chicken now, or what?"

"Ee-e-e! *Ee-e-e-e-e-e-e!*"

———   ———   ———   ———   ———

Brennan's mother returned home right after his room inspection, so, for the second time that week, the timing allowed for them to all sit down and eat together as a family.

She was extra quiet and reserved around her son when she first arrived, scurrying about the house, transitioning from *work-mode* to *home-mode* while avoiding eye-contact with him whenever the two of them shared the same room, and responding to him only in curt, clipped phrases and sounds like "*Mm,*" and "*Nn-nn,*" and "*Yep... I'm fine... Just... Fine...*"

She had been that way with him ever since his outburst with her at the dinner table a couple nights ago. But once the father told Brennan to take her back and show her the work he did in his bedroom, she finally began relaxing and warming up to him again, as the three prepared to sit down for dinner.

—   —   —   —   —

"I really hope the two of you savor this meal..." The father said to the other two, sitting down with his plate and drink. "This measly little fast-food feast alone cost me half a day's pay. Just for a basic fried chicken dinner and sides—I mean, *incredible...*"

The dinner itself was, of course, delicious, and the three of them spent another evening joking, laughing, and fully enjoying each other's company, without any trace of fear or irritation.

—   —   —   —   —

When Friday came, Brennan got up, showered, heated up a plate of the previous night's leftovers for his breakfast, then went back to his room to play video games while he waited for his parents to wake up.

They both ended up sleeping in until the early afternoon, as they often did on their work days. Still half-asleep and shuffling around the house in his bathrobe, groaning and rubbing his face while he waited for his coffee to brew, the father had all but forgotten that Brennan was still home for the week. After tasting his first steaming hot sip of coffee, he turned around to find Brennan sitting quietly at the table, smiling his normal big, friendly smile, then throwing his hand up, fingers spread as wide as they could go, and waving it around with blurry speed, saying, "Good *morning!* What we doing today, father-sir?"

The greeting was so chipper, and so jarring to the man's freshly-woken mind, that his startled jolt made the coffee leap up from the lip of his mug and come splashing down onto his hand

and dribbling a little onto the floor.

"Ooh, *hot! Hot-hot-hot... Ah-ah-ah-ah-aaaah...!*" he said, spinning around to set the mug back down on the counter, shaking the residual coffee drops off his hand, and then running his hand under the faucet. He turned back to face his son and sighed, saying, "...Well, *good morning* to you, too! Still not used to you being here in the mornings... *Apparently*... But, let's see... What to do, what to *do-o-o...?*"

The father checked the time and only had a little over an hour before he needed to leave, so he said, "Well, I still gotta get myself ready for work, but why don't we put our heads together and try to think of some ways you can make yourself useful today, huh? So, you keep thinking of productive ways you can spend your day, and I'll do the same while I finish getting ready, alright? Then we'll meet back here and share what we came up with. Sound good?"

"Sounds good!"

So, Brennan grabbed a sheet of paper and a pencil from his father's office and began writing out his list, and when the man returned to join him at the table—showered, shaved, and with his own reheated plate of leftovers-for-breakfast—he stuffed a forkful of food into his cheek and, between his bites, said, "So... Whatcha got for me? Lay it on me."

"Oh. Well... You said that you were gonna come up with some ideas, too, so the only things I came up with were: *Clean my room again*—but I crossed that one out because it still looks pretty good, I think—then it's just, *Do more jump ropes, do more push-ups, and do more jumping jacks...* What did you come up with?"

The father set down his fork, wiped his mouth with a napkin, and finished his bite before saying, "*Uhh,* well, *no,* what I actually *said*—if you'll remember—was that *I* would go and get myself ready while *you* would sit here and write out a list of ideas."

"No, but you said—"

"—Don't argue with me, son... You've been on a good streak, and I don't want to see you break it now..."

"Yes, sir, father-sir."

The man checked his watch. "Anyway, uhh... *Yeah*, I think we can probably pump a little iron in the garage before I gotta take off. If you wanna go get set up and let me scarf down my food here, then I'll go meet you out there when I'm done. Sound good?"

"Sounds good!"

Brennan sprinted out to the garage, turned the lights on, and searched through their tub of exercise equipment for his jump rope. Next to the rope, he found a pair of his mother's pink, rubber-coated dumbbells that looked just his size, so he grabbed those as well and spent his remaining time doing bicep curls on his father's workbench, absent-mindedly singing the theme song to *Just The 3 Of Us* to himself while he waited.

When his father eventually came out and found his son singing to himself in a high falsetto voice, he winced at the sight, removing the pink weights from the boy with delicate fingers, as though he were handling sticks of dynamite. "Alright, *macho man*, I'm glad to see you taking some initiative with your fitness here, but, uh... Those are your *mother's* weights. *Girls'* weights. Next time you wanna lift some weights, *tell me*, and I'm sure I can find you something that looks a little less... *Prissy*. And we can probably find you some better music to work out to as well." He spoke a couple commands into the air, and a robotic voice answered, then began playing some loud rock song that Brennan had never heard before. "So, whatcha say, champ? You ready to try those push-ups again?"

Brennan did better with his push-ups that day, completing five of the *'easy'* push-ups on his knees before he had to stop, then he moved on to several more minutes of jump rope and jumping jacks until his cheeks flushed a blotchy pink and his short hair was all weighed down and shining slick with sweat. His father told him to try giving push-ups one more go, but after giving it his best effort, the boy collapsed to the floor on his second push—thus concluding his exercise for the day.

They closed up the garage and Brennan bid his father a nice day at work, waving him goodbye as he watched the man's truck get smaller and smaller until it disappeared down the street.

Back inside, Brennan bumped into his mother in the hallway—her make-up only half-done, eye-liner pencil in-hand—who was buzzing about from room-to-room in her usual pre-work multi-tasking frenzy. "Morning, sweetie—*oof!* What happened to *you?* You look—" she sniffed at his damp hair, "—oh, *gawd!*—and *smell* like you just walked out of a *sweatshop!*"

Brennan laughed. "Oh, I was just out in the garage, uhh... You know... *'Pumping metal'* with father."

"*'Pumping metal,'* huh? Well, uhh... Y'might wanna think about taking a shower or something, because, *erm...*" Her eyes darted all about the hallway, distracted, muttering, '*ers*' and '*uhs*' to herself as she navigated the chaos of her own swirling thoughts, trying to recall what her next step was supposed to be, when they both heard the microwave ding. "Oh, *duh*—the *food!* God, I still haven't even *eaten* yet and I'm already running behind—well, that's just *great.* Hey, uh, sweetie, actually, if you're gonna talk to me, how 'bout we walk-and-talk, yeah?"

Brennan followed her to the kitchen where she pulled her plate of leftovers from the microwave, only then noticing the eyeliner pencil she still carried clutched in her hand, cursing at the realization. "Aw, *great*—now I can't even *eat.* Tell you what, honey, could you do your mommy a *hu-u-uge* favor and pack this up for me in, like, a to-go container? With a fork? I still gotta finish getting ready and I'm already running late."

"Yeah, yeah—you go, mommy! You finish getting ready—I got this!"

"*Ugh*—you're an *angel!*" She kissed him on the forehead and dashed back to her room.

Brennan, meanwhile, searched through the lower cupboards until he found a big-enough container and a lid to match it. He raised her plate and dumped its contents, tumbling and slopping, into the plastic tub, then he scraped the remaining streaks of macaroni, potatoes, and gravy into the container with a fork. He had to cram the lid on tight to get it to stay on, forcing all of its squishier contents up against the walls and lid, but he was just barely able to seal the lid on tight before it started oozing over the sides. Then he packed it all up in a grocery bag, remembering to throw in the fork before tying it shut, and he waited with the bag, by the living room entrance.

A few minutes later, his mother's door flew open and she stormed out of the room, snatching her scarf off the rack, slipping on her sunglasses, and racing for the front door. "Hey, love-you, sweetie—sorry I can't chat this morning, but I *really* gotta go; *you have a great day though!* Number's on the fridge if there's an emergency—gotta go, *bye!*" And without even glancing in the boy's direction, she ran right past him and out the door.

Brennan smirked, recognizing the oblivious scene from countless movies and TV shows. He counted down from five, out loud, holding the bag at a stiff arm's length, expecting her to burst back in—recalling, in her frazzled tizzy, the lunch that she'd asked him to pack—plucking the bag from his hand with a funny quip before dashing back out the door.

But once he had finished his countdown and didn't hear the click-clack of her steps scuffling back up the path, he scurried out to the doorstep and found her next to her SUV, clawing through her purse in a wild-eyed frenzy.

He curved his free hand around his mouth and called out to her. "Mommy! Hey, over *here! Mommy—Wait!*"

She spun around, huffing and rolling her eyes to the sky at *yet another* obstacle in her morning's path—that is, until she saw the bag in his hand and heard the words: *Your food.*

Brennan ran out in his socks to meet her halfway, where she snatched the bag out of his hands, saying, "Oh, that's right, *yeah-yeah-yeah*—thanks, sweetie—okay, gotta go, *by-y-e-e!*"

He made his way back into the house leaping from tiptoe to tiptoe like a ballet dancer—trying not to get his socks too dirty or step on any bugs or snails along the path—then he turned and waved to her from the doorway as she got in the SUV and drove off, unsure if she saw him waving or not, before heading back inside and locking the door behind him.

As neither he nor his father could think up any new tasks to keep him busy while his parents were at work, Brennan was left with the rest of the day to himself, to spend however he chose. Naturally, he decided to spend the day stretched out on his bed, relaxing and playing video games.

He was so engrossed in his game that he completely forgot to make himself lunch, and the time passed so quickly that when his father arrived home first that evening, Brennan's first thought was that somebody must be breaking into their house. Then he heard the man's voice, powered-down his game, and came rushing out to meet him.

—　　　—　　　—　　　—　　　—

Throughout that night's dinner, and all through the rest of their weekend, the whole family managed to get along without a hitch. The parents still spent a lot of their time complaining about their work days—both to their son and to each other—but the only miseries and frustrations that came up in conversation were the ones they brought with them from outside of their home.

Brennan didn't have the words to express all of the *goodness* he felt throughout that weekend. And it wasn't just the friendly, tension-free ways they treated him whenever their paths crossed in the house, nor was it merely their whimsical family adventures to the movie theater on Saturday night and the city zoo for the better part of their Sunday. Both were gleeful bonding events for Brennan and his parents, filled with snacks, souvenirs, and laughter, that would echo on in their memories for years as a shining example of '*the good times*'—not so remarkable for the rarity of such weekend family adventures, but for how rarely those outings ever ended with everyone returning home still tear-free and feeling good.

There was a palpable change in the air those last few days. He saw it in their faces whenever they lit up laughing at each other's jokes and silliness. He heard it in the quiet murmur of the TV coming from his parents' room at night, punctuated by bursts of their combined laughter. He felt it lying in bed at night, with his whole body stretched out and relaxed—healed enough from Tuesday's discipline session to sleep peacefully and relatively pain-free throughout the night on his back—and even felt it as he awoke, meeting the day with a sense of calm and well-rested focus in the still morning, hours before either of his parents awoke.

For the first time since before Brennan started the fifth grade, he finally felt like he, his life, and his family were all back on the right track—the way they should be.

Everything just felt… *All better*, somehow.

Lying in his bed that Sunday night, he reflected back on which recent developments had played the biggest parts in fixing his life so quickly. He would have, for sure, been in big trouble if his parents knew that he had spent most of Thursday, and *all* of Friday, playing video games. But when his father called, Brennan was clever enough to tell a harmless little lie—one that didn't even hurt anybody or make anybody feel bad—and he got away with it (even if he did feel so anxious he thought he would pass out). Then, of course, there was also Tuesday's discipline session with the belt, which Brennan figured must have been the *main* thing that kept him good and out of trouble for the rest of that week—well… *Mostly* good, anyway… Except for that one *lie* he told… But he didn't even get in any trouble for that one, so he didn't think it really counted. But the one recent thing that had definitely *never* happened before, was him starting an actual *fight* at school—*with kids cheering and recording it on their phones and everything!*

If he had just left that new kid alone and didn't bother telling him what a stupid little liar he really is… Then, really… *None* of the good stuff that was happening would have happened.

Without that fight at school, his parents would still be mad all the time. They'd still say mean things at each other, *and* at him. He *definitely* wouldn't have had any free time to do any of the fun stuff he got to do. No, instead, he just would've been camped out in the dining room with his books and papers scattered all over the table, bored to a drained and lifeless husk under a mountain of Mr Q's homework—yet still racing to finish it all before, once again, passing out at the table from exhaustion.

He knew that there were *other* people who believed that his fight with the new kid was wrong. *Most* people probably did. His parents were the biggest ones—*even though they probably hate that new kid just as much as I do*, he thought—but there was also the security lady, the office secretary, that big girl with the pigtails, probably, and *obviously* the new kid himself... But the more he rolled these thoughts around in his mind, the more it seemed to him that his actions were not only '*not*-wrong', but actually kind of '*good*', and maybe even the *right* thing to do.

He remembered what his parents had told him at the start of that week, about how *nobody's ever really good; they only care about looking good*. The idea was still a little difficult for Brennan to fully wrap his mind around—as he felt certain that he had met some truly good, caring people in his lifetime—but he shook off his doubts, repeating their words as his own, over and over in his head, certain that, if he could only make sense of his parents' wisdom, then it would help him unravel the mystery behind all of his recent good feelings, and learn how he could keep them going without any further backsliding.

Maybe they meant that, like, nobody will ever be as good and as nice as that one famous Jesus guy that they put up on the cross, so there's really no point in pretending that we'll ever actually be as perfectly good as Him. Or, maybe, they just meant that, like, it doesn't even really matter all that much if we do bad, selfish stuff sometimes, as long as we still feel *like we're a good person on the* inside—*since that's where all of the real important stuff is anyway.*

Brennan didn't exactly *want* to do bad things. Even the times when he was bad or did bad stuff, he never really *wanted* to be bad. He liked being nice and friendly, helping out whenever he could, and making people feel good, and—*for the most part*—he felt bad if he ever put someone down or said mean things. But if that weekend had taught him anything, it was that, if he could sometimes be willing to do just a *little bit* of bad stuff, from time to time—and only ever for the things he *really* wanted, or the times when he was feeling *extra* sad or angry, or if a little white lie might help him avoid trouble, and *definitely* only if it seemed like things would work out okay afterward—well, then maybe those so-called 'bad' things could actually make things a little better, or easier, or happier for himself. And judging by his parents' sunnier dispositions over that week, a little bit of bad stuff might even make things better for everyone around him as well.

Just like Vengeance Man.

Brennan knew that he didn't have it all figured out a hundred-percent just yet, but he reasoned that he was still little, and he'd still have plenty of time to figure the rest of it out as he got older and smarter.

For now though, little Brennan had convinced himself that he was onto something—something *big* that even the new kid wasn't smart enough to understand.

Eleven.

The next morning, Brennan woke before his alarm went off and got himself dressed, fed, and ready as usual for his big day back to school. And as usual, his parents were both still sound asleep by the time he embarked on his morning commute. But unlike most days, Brennan left his house that chilly morning skipping along the sidewalk with a warm smile on his face. He felt so good that he wanted to sing, but the only song he really knew all the words to and still enjoyed singing was the *Just The 3 Of Us* theme song, and he just couldn't bring himself to sing that song ever again—as just the thought of all those *liars* and *phoneys* was enough to make him *sick-to-his-stomach*—so instead, he decided to sing one of the new songs that his father played in the garage, but as he could only remember the funny chorus of one of the songs, he just repeated that simple line— *"Yeah! Yeah! Dude looks like a lay-day…"*—over and over as he danced down the street, feeling great about the day.

His father had set him straight and Brennan knew that he was finally ready to be good at school again—and if he absolutely *had to* do something that was just *kinda bad…* Well, then he knew how to do it a little better now, *without* getting into trouble. But he felt pretty sure that he wouldn't have to. He would be *good.* He would do all of his work and stay quiet in class and not get into any more fights—not unless that new kid was stupid enough to start any more trouble with *him.* And if he did, then Brennan would be ready for him—careful to watch out for any of his tricky, cheap moves.

He was the first student to arrive in Mr. Q's classroom— as was often the case—and he debated with himself as to whether or not he should disturb Mr. Q at his desk to ask about the previous week's homework, or if he should wait for a better opportunity. But upon entering, his feet made the decision for him, veering him directly back toward his seat the moment he saw Mr. Q's silhouette hunched behind his laptop screen.

Just before he got to his seat, however, he was stopped by the sound of the man's voice, saying, "You there... *Boy*... You were absent from my class all last week, yes?"

"Oh, uh, yes, sir. There was a thing where I got in a little trouble because I—"

"—Yes, yes, I'm sure there was a reason—even *if* I couldn't care any less—but the only reason I ask is so you can start getting yourself up to speed on the work you missed. Here, *come...*" When Brennan shuffled up to Mr. Q's desk, the man reached into a deep desk drawer and pulled out a stack of four paperback novels, dropping them down in front of Brennan, with a resonant *clap*, on the corner of his desk. "There, now. You will take these books home with you, you will read them in a timely manner— *timely*, that is, for someone who abandoned their schooling responsibilities for the better part of a week—and then you will write me a five-page report on each. This will all, of course, be expected of you by Friday, turned in alongside all of *this* week's homework assignments as well. That is all. You may go now."

Brennan nodded and returned to his seat carrying the stack of four books wedged under his trembling chin. All of those nice, peaceful feelings that filled his heart when he left the house that morning had dried up, evaporated into a wisp of vapor, replaced now by a whirlpool of spiraling anxiety.

He sat, gnawing on the end of his pen, gently rocking himself back and forth in his desk seat, trying to figure out how he was going to finish two weeks' worth of work within the next three-and-a-half days, hardly aware at all of the sight and sounds of his peers pouring in and taking their seats all around him. But when Mr Q rose to take the morning attendance and began calling out their names, Brennan's attention snapped him back to where he was, clasping his hands on his desk, raising his heels and digging his toes into the floor to keep them from tapping. After he heard his own name called out and replied, he turned in his seat to glance back at the new kid, but found his seat as vacant and gaping as the dark red hole a tooth leaves behind.

"*Right...*" Mr. Q said, addressing the class once he had finished his roll call, "So, first-things-first, as those of you with a knack for names and faces might recall, last Monday, we welcomed a new child into our classroom. His *name* escapes me at the moment, but regardless, this boy had supposedly tested well enough to allow him to skip the fourth grade entirely. *Ring any bells?* Well, I do hope that none of you were looking forward to becoming new '*besties*' with the lad because—as I might well have predicted—the banal expectations of the fifth grade must have proved too rigorous for even *his* staggering nine-year-old intellect, as—apparently—after only a mere day-and-a-half amongst *you* animals, his parents decided to pluck him from our happy classroom and pursue their son's education elsewhere—" then he muttered, loud enough for all the students in the first couple rows to hear him, "*—and I can't exactly say I* blame *them either, I mean, just* look *at the sorry lot of you... It's like you were raised by wolves, some of you—or perhaps even* baser *creatures... —Oh!* And I should add that word has also gotten back to me that one of you rotten little miscreants managed to *brutalize* the poor child last week. Now, while I don't know *which* one of you it was—nor do I particularly *care*—I do wish to make myself nice and sparkling clear when I tell you all that *we will have no more of that in my classroom.* Now, have I made myself understood?"

The class responded in a variety of loud, droning affirmatives, their voices all sloppily overlapping and dissolving into one another, morphing into a single cacophonous noise that reached Mr. Q's ears sounding like: *UH-HMM-HUH-YEH-HESS-SURR-ESS-MISSER-QUEWSER.*

The man's lips pulled down into an ugly, pained wince, shaking his head as fast as a wet dog, like he was trying to shake out the last echoes of their voices. "*Wonderful...* Now, we've already wasted too many minutes of our day discussing the fate of a child who's not even our problem anymore, so, with that business swiftly out of the way and off our minds, let us quickly pick up where we were on Friday's discussion of last week's reading, shall we? Now, as you *should* all remember—*if* you were paying attention—we last left off discussing the climactic breakdown of our protagonist's interior exploration, and even his *renunciation*, of his entire life's belief system up to that point, and during the middle of his big third-act soliloquy, where he begins to adopt the perspective of his opponent, who—up until this point in the story..."

Wait... Brennan thought, *Di-did I just hear him right? Could the new kid... Is he really gone—like, gone, gone—just like that? This is all... It's just... It really is kinda just like Vengeance Man! What was it that mommy said at dinner last week? Something like... 'Breaking the law and hurting people is okay sometimes, as long it means helping all the good, regular people and sending the bad guys away'...? Well, that's exactly what I did. Me. I did it. I got rid of that stupid, mean liar, all by myself, and now he's gone forever. Now he won't be able to make any of us regular kids sad ever again with his stupid big-mouth lies. And maybe someone at his next school will also stand up to him and make him shut up and tell the truth, and then he'll have to go to another school... And another school... And more and more schools until he either stops lying or he finally ends up in jail... And it's all because of me... Because I did a so-called 'bad' thing... But I guess, sometimes, being bad and doing bad stuff can still end up making good stuff happen, too... Maybe even a lot of good stuff—like all the good stuff from this week...*

And in those few moments, with the dawning of those new realizations, some exciting new shape began to take root deep down within Brennan—deeper, even, than his words or thinking mind could go, down to a place just beneath his feelings and emotions. And it spoke to him, this sprouting shape, telling him things that made him feel *bigger*, somehow. Stronger. Smarter. Like his thoughts and opinions suddenly *mattered* more. Like *he* mattered more.

And before long, the voice of this blossoming entity became the guiding influence behind many of his decision-making processes. Whether lying to his teacher, on a predictable weekly basis, about why his homework assignments were never complete, or lying to his parents about... Well, *anything*, really, if he felt that the truth might land him in trouble. And even when he *did* get busted from time to time—however harsh his punishment was—he could always trust that, whatever decisions he made or lies he told under the guidance of that new voice growing inside him, he would *still* be in better shape than if he had simply told the truth, welcoming all the pain and punishment that so predictably followed.

Little by little, conflict after conflict, month after month, and year after year, this entity continued growing inside of Brennan, developing until it was the exact same size and shape inside of him as his body looked on the outside.

Whenever he was alone with his thoughts or feeling contemplative, it was this spectral inner-entity who provided Brennan with a dazzling variety of thoughts, opinions, and attitudes that could take his mind off of whatever was troubling him. Whenever Brennan spoke, it was the entity's words and tone of voice that people heard coming out of his mouth.

And he liked the way its voice sounded.

Its voice came to him a thousand times quieter than a whisper, and though its tone only ever seemed to alternate between fearful and judgmental, it was always there for him when he needed a little help feeling better, making him feel good and right and strong during times when he would have otherwise felt quite small, or sad about his life and who he was. It helped him come up with clever, funny things to say about his teachers and peers behind their backs—and sometimes, even to their faces—working his classmates up into hollering fits of laughter. It even started helping him figure out things to say during the times he felt angriest toward his parents—granted, *those* things he said would often end in tears or even more yelling, depending on who he talked back to, but he always felt a *little bit* better about his punishments after saying some especially mean or hurtful thing that got under their skin. And since he never had to *lie* when he snapped back at his parents, he didn't even have to feel like he was doing anything 'bad' or 'wrong'. *He simply told them the truth of how he felt about them; it wasn't his fault if they couldn't handle it.*

The more he listened to that mesmerizing voice, the more it fascinated him—like a defenseless, developing mind sucked into the ecstatic lights and sounds of a personal screen—and the more convinced he grew that he and this phantom developing inside of him were, in fact, *one* entity. This was an easy enough oversight for the boy, as he could scarcely remember a time when that fiercely protective and judgmental inner-voice wasn't keeping him safe and smart and funny and cool and—for the *most* part—out of trouble.

As far as Brennan was concerned, it had always been with him.

And he trusted that it always would be.

—   —   —   —   —

While Brennan's life story *ultimately* ends well, many years later—both for him and the people in his life who love him—he spent far too many decades of his life allowing that always-chattering voice inside him to call the shots, influencing his every thought, word, belief, and action, believing the lie that he had ever needed to heed the demands of that poor, frightened voice within him in the first place.

Fortunately, like all those who commit themselves to unlearning the harmful beliefs they once held true, Brennan, too, was eventually able to awaken from that voice's spell and live his life freely once again. But, as is too often the case, he first had to lose everything he valued and cared about in his life before he could make the choice to explore the depths of that hazardous inner-space for himself.

For now, however, this early chapter of Brennan's story has reached its conclusion.

The next chapter of his tale will be a different story... For another time...

Dedication

I dedicate this book to our world's young people—past, present, and future:

All you inexperienced and powerless masses, bursting with limitless potential—who, throughout all of known history, have been forced to endure and adapt to the ways of the adults who govern their early lives—regardless of how immature or ignorant they might be in their perspectives, or how clumsy or cruel their displays of affection, however hardened or otherwise mistaken their ways might be...

To any young person who might read this, please know this and take it with you forever:

There will always *be those of us—even when you can't see us—who have dedicated their lives, and are working hard, to build a better future for you. Please, keep going, for as long as you possibly can, and always do what you can to help make this world a better, safer, more loving place for everyone.*

And to Sophia, specifically:

You were so loved by so many, kiddo, and you left us all way too soon. I miss you every day, now and forever, and I hope you hear us talking to you, wherever you are.